DEATH

by Education

DEATH
by Education

Marion Rosen

St. Martin's Press
New York

ISBN 0-312-09268-7

First Edition: June 1993

10 9 8 7 6 5 4 3 2 1

This book is dedicated to the memory of three people who believed in me long before I believed in myself:

Howard C. Spannuth, my father
Dora K. Spannuth, my mother
Lucile Anne Gardner, my friend

Acknowledgments

My sincere thanks to Barry A. J. Fisher, director of the Los Angeles County Sheriff's crime laboratory, for his advice and assistance, and to Officer Stanley Weidenhaupt of the Foothill Division of the Los Angeles Police Department for his willingness to answer my questions in spite of his busy schedule.

Thanks also to my most helpful and supportive readers who kept me on track: Morrie Rosen, Marylou Mahar, Doris Haase, Linda Ruhle, Ruth Glean Rosing, LaVonne Taylor-Pickell, Linda Jameson, Kristine O'Connell George, April Halprin Wayland, and Barney Saltzberg.

Most of all I am grateful for the love and enthusiasm of Ann Garrett, Karen Vik Eustis, and Abby Yolles for their wisdom, which is always tempered with kindness.

1

GRETA Gallagher drove her five-year-old Toyota through the open chain-link gate and into the service drive that bisected the McCormick High campus. Being a teacher and counselor was hard enough on sunny days, but this was one of those overcast October mornings when the low clouds seemed to cling to the rooftops of the one-story buildings scattered Los Angeles style across the sprawling grounds.

Later in the day the haze would probably give way to sunshine, but the air at seven o'clock was still damp, chilling Greta even inside the car. Oh, well, at least it was Friday, and she could feel virtuous about having fought off the urge to call in sick and spend the morning in bed.

Her arms felt heavy against the steering wheel; a little stiffness crept across her shoulders. Maybe she was spending too many late-night hours watching "The Tonight Show." She decided no TV tonight. Wait, tonight began the weekend. She'd mend her ways come Sunday.

Greta pulled into the parking lot—actually just a paved area between two bungalows used as classrooms. She turned off the engine, hoisted her purse and book bag from the floor next to her, and flicked a speck of lint from the front of her navy blue skirt.

Was this the fifth or sixth year she'd worn this same skirt to work? Her school wardrobe desperately needed a lift, but she'd just paid for a tune-up and a new timing belt for the car. Maybe after the next paycheck she'd treat herself to a shopping spree. Then again, at today's prices she'd settle for a new outfit or two.

Greta smoothed her hand over her tawny, shoulder-length pageboy, tucking a stray wisp of hair back into place. She had remembered lipstick, the only makeup she ever wore, and she checked the car's side mirror for pink smudges on her teeth. Why she went through this ritual she wasn't sure, because no one was ever around to notice how she looked. The teachers who arrived early usually sequestered themselves, like an army under siege, in one of the two faculty lounges or in the teachers' cafeteria.

She crossed the campus in long, brisk strides, her shoulder bag bumping against her hip. Crumpled notebook paper and food wrappers blew around her feet, skittering in little eddies until they stuck like wallpaper against a fence or lodged in a doorway. Just before she entered the main building that housed the counseling and administrative offices, a gust of wind made a mess of her hair. She combed it away from her eyes with her fingers, wishing she'd used a bit of hair spray that morning.

The counseling office, a dingy gray-green room, cast a flood of fluorescent light into the main corridor. No sign of the four other counselors. Why was she always the first to arrive and the last to leave? Maybe she should listen to her friend Maxine Kramer, who also acted as the school's union rep, and forget about being a supercounselor, especially since the school district's bureaucracy never seemed to notice her dedication, much less reward it. In fact, the smiles and thanks she got from the students were her only rewards aside from the anemic paychecks. If it weren't for the kids, she'd have bailed out long ago.

Vera Campbell, the office secretary, pursed her lips and squinted at Greta over the horn-rimmed granny glasses perched on the tip of her nose. "Fran won't be in today. She asked if you could cover any problems that come up. Lord knows I'll barely have time to take messages for her."

All business, that was Vera. Most of the counselors put up with Vera's curtness because she was efficient at her job, but they also treated her more or less like a piece of office furniture.

"Okay," Greta said with a sigh. A sub—if they could get one—would take over Fran Elliot's two American History classes, but any problems regarding Fran's half of the senior class would be Greta's today.

"And you had a call," Vera said. "Mrs. Jackson. She's frantic because her daughter never came home after cheerleading practice yesterday. Out the whole night somewhere. The poor woman's worried sick—"

"Wait, do you mean Belinda? Belinda Jackson?"

"Yeah, that's the one. I wrote everything down. Memo's on your desk."

"That isn't like Belinda. Did Mrs. Jackson call the police?"

Vera raised one penciled eyebrow. "Police won't find her if she's holed up somewhere with her boyfriend."

Greta hurried into the cubicle that served as her private office. Though it was hardly big enough for a desk and a few chairs, unlike some of the other offices her little niche did have a bit of natural light. Her scrawny collection of plants lined the narrow windowsill, and a collage of photographs of former students and counselees concealed the peeling paint on one wall. A few of those faces she could no longer connect with names, but she did remember the faces, at least the way they had looked in high school.

At the beginning of the semester—which thanks to year-round scheduling now began in August—Greta had returned to work with some hope that, in her two hours of teaching English and her counseling sessions the rest of the day, she could make a difference. But as usual, reality set in after a few weeks.

3

Though she did what she could for her students, in most cases it didn't even come close to the kind of help they needed.

This was the last day of the semester's ninth week, and already problems took up most of her day. Just yesterday a pregnant student had cried her eyes out in Greta's arms, and she had suspended two boys for fighting and bringing switchblades onto the campus.

And now Belinda, one of the few good ones, was missing.

She flipped through the three-hundred-plus cards in her file box of student schedule programs until she came to Belinda's name. She dialed the number on the card, carefully printed in Belinda's own hand.

The hello came before the end of the first ring.

"Mrs. Jackson, this is Greta Gallagher at McCormick. Have you heard from Belinda?"

"No. Something terrible has happened. I just know it."

"Don't worry," Greta said, "she'll turn up. Belinda probably spent the night at a girlfriend's house and forgot to tell you."

"Belinda always comes right home after school. Always. I was so sure she'd show up, I waited until almost eleven last night before I called the police."

Greta could almost hear the woman's lips trembling. "Did the police check the hospitals?"

"Yes, but so far there's no sign of her."

"I'll check to see if she shows up for her first-period class, then I'll call you. Please try not to worry."

Greta hung up and checked Belinda's program card: Period one, Algebra II, Room 26.

She walked to the counter separating the student waiting area from the counselors' work space. Methodically, Vera was filling out a form, readmitting a student who had been absent the day before.

"Vera," Greta called, "hold down the fort for a minute, will you? I have to run over to my classroom to get a book."

Vera muttered something under her breath. The student, probably a tenth-grader, looked up at Greta. "Well, get a move on," Vera said. "I can't do all the readmits by myself."

Greta felt her face redden and hurried into the corridor so Vera wouldn't notice. Vera had set herself up as a one-woman patrol, a watchdog to ensure that the counselors didn't waste any time goofing off. Vera certainly wasn't in charge of office procedures—the head counselor took care of operations, and of course the principal handled personnel—but apparently no one had ever explained this to Vera. At times Vera's officiousness bugged the hell out of Greta, but she'd long ago decided against trying to set Vera straight.

She headed for the room she shared with Cecelia Hartman in the English building. Now there was another one who could stand a few weeks of charm school. Crabbier than hell most days and just plain grouchy on the rest, Cecelia had earned the nickname Dragon Lady among the students. The kids probably had a few other names for Cecelia they never used in front of Greta.

The campus was still deserted. Except for the handful of students involved in band practice, most arrived just moments before the eight o'clock bell. Those who couldn't even handle sliding into place just under the wire—the habitually tardy—would show up sometime before nine. Greta already had a stack of notes on her desk regarding seniors who had three tardies. It was going to be a long, hard winter.

She unlocked the door to room 43 and, without turning on the light, grabbed her copy of the American Lit book from the teacher's desk. If no major problems surfaced in the counseling office during period one, she might have time to prepare some questions for her fourth- and fifth-period classes. She might even kick off a discussion that would wake up sleepers like Bryan and Garland and make them forget they had to work at jobs that paid less than minimum wage until eleven or sometimes even midnight on school nights.

Who was she trying to kid? With or without thought-provoking questions, the kids would no more be prepared to analyze *The Scarlet Letter* than they would be ready to discuss nuclear physics. Still, she had to go through the motions. She'd be damned if she'd give in to the apathy running rampant among the other teachers.

She pushed the door open just as a boy outside kicked his locker shut. The loud slam echoed harshly between the buildings.

"Aww," the boy groaned when he spotted her. "Busted." He waited for his punishment, staring at the ground.

Greta closed the door and looked at him. He carried an instrument case, probably for a clarinet. "You new here?"

"Nah."

"Then you already know we expect you to take better care of school property?"

"Yeah, I know, it was just that . . ."

"Just that you didn't expect to get caught?"

The boy almost grinned. "I'm sorry. I'll close it right next time."

"Thanks. Now get out of here before I change my mind about reporting this."

The boy broke into a run and disappeared around a corner. Funny how each year, as the big problems grew in seriousness, the minor ones became easier and easier to overlook.

Greta started walking back to her office, then noticed that the door to the English teachers' workroom wasn't latched tightly. Damn. It was ajar only a fraction of an inch, but an unlocked door left the room vulnerable to vandals.

Cecelia Hartman, who was also head of the English department, would have a fit. Greta shuddered to think of Cecelia's ordered files dumped on the floor, or worse yet, covered with paint or glue. Maybe the custodian hadn't locked the door properly; perhaps there was no damage at all, but Greta knew the odds.

She touched the knob before she discovered why the door hadn't closed. Something was lying on the floor, blocking the door open. Something black.

The object on the floor could've been almost anything, but since the workroom had no windows, she couldn't see clearly. She opened the door a few inches, enough to let the foggy gray daylight illuminate the problem. Then she saw that the thing wedged in the doorway was the toe of a black tennis shoe.

She sensed rather than saw something terribly wrong. She pulled the door open a few more inches, her hand shaking as she reached inside for the light switch. It seemed a lifetime before the overhead fluorescent tubes flickered on, drenching the tiny room in yellow brilliance. The granola she'd eaten for breakfast rose halfway up her throat, stifling her scream.

Greta held the door open with one outstretched hand and edged sideways into the room, trying not to get too close. She sucked in a deep breath, then was immediately sorry. The air was stuffy, heavy with a disagreeable odor. As hard as she tried, she couldn't shift her eyes away from the sight on the floor.

She had found Belinda Jackson.

2

GRETA tried to concentrate, tried to think. Somewhere in a recess of her brain she must have stored away the correct procedure, what the school district would want her to do in a case like this, but her mind drew a blank. Her muscles tightened; her stomach cramped into a fiery lump.

Greta stepped all the way into the room and leaned over the girl. How could this ashen face—these blank, staring eyes—belong to Belinda? The girl wore her red-and-black cheerleaders' outfit, but she looked younger, smaller than Greta remembered. What had happened to the bouncy, vibrant girl who had always tried so hard to please?

Greta touched the soft cheek for a second, then withdrew her hand. Should she check the girl's pulse? No. No need to confirm what she already knew.

For some reason, Greta did not want to leave Belinda alone. She inched over to the unreliable old rotary phone, praying she would hear a dial tone. Thank God. The mechanical buzz hummed loudly in her ear. She dialed nine for an outside line, then slowly spun out nine-one-one.

By now her mind had somehow detached from the horror of what must have taken place, and she reported her gruesome discovery mechanically. She gave the police the school's address and mentioned the nearest cross streets. This was the police, for God's sake. Surely they knew how to find the school, but she gave them directions anyway. It was not painful to talk about cross streets. After the police assured her that help was on the way, Greta dialed the principal's office.

"Good morning." A familiar masculine voice.

"Adam, it's Greta Gallagher. I'm in the English workroom. I just found one of our students, Belinda Jackson. Adam, she's dead."

Adam Mason did not respond immediately. When he finally spoke, his voice was calm. "Where exactly is she? Are you sure she's dead?"

"Yes, she's right here on the floor next to me. Her mother reported her missing. I called nine-one-one, but I didn't know what to do next."

"Don't do anything. I'll be right there."

Greta replaced the receiver and knelt next to the girl's left hand. Two of Belinda's shiny red fingernails were broken, ragged. Good for you, Belinda. At least you fought back. Not that it did any good.

Belinda was different from most of the other kids. In her junior year, she'd worked in Greta's office, filing and running errands, so Greta had gotten to know her better than she knew most of the students. Belinda was not only mature for her years but sensitive as well. She actually got upset when she had an overdue library book, and she really cared about saving the whales. Belinda was what was known in the business as a good kid. Greta spent so much of her time with the kids who had problems that she seldom became really close to the good ones, except for a few. Belinda was one of the few.

Greta bit her lip. The girl stared straight ahead at a spot that must have been where her murderer had stood. His face would have been the last thing Belinda saw before those dark eyes went empty. A madman. Greta shivered.

Why was Adam taking so long? She couldn't stand Belinda's

staring for another second. She bent over and touched the girl's eyelids. She pressed, gently at first, then more firmly, until the flesh slid down over Belinda's eyes. That was better. Belinda looked almost peaceful now.

Greta heard footsteps outside, then a voice. "Wait out here. Right there, by the wall." She stood up.

Adam opened the door a crack, looked in, focused on Belinda. "Oh, my God." He stepped inside and pulled the door shut.

Greta walked over to the principal and stood there speechless. Adam shook his head but didn't look at Greta. He couldn't seem to take his eyes off the fallen girl.

Tears began rolling down Greta's cheeks.

"I'm sorry, let me get you out of here," Adam whispered.

Greta nodded. Why did people always whisper around the dead? Just in case they might be able to hear us after all?

Adam said, "I'll get some of the phys ed teachers to close off the gates before the kids start wandering around. I also have to put in a call to the superintendent. I can do it from here while I wait for the police."

Greta nodded again, wiped her eyes. Adam put his arm around her shoulders and steered her outside. He whispered, "I brought Maxine along." To Maxine he said, "Take Greta to my office. Stay there with her until I get back, no matter how long it takes."

Adam slipped back into the workroom and closed the door. A confused-looking Maxine was standing off to the side, leaning against the lockers.

"Are you all right? What's going on? You look awful," Maxine said.

Greta took a few steps toward Maxine, then stopped. How did you explain something like this?

"What the hell is going on around here?" Maxine didn't

10

wait for an answer, but then she seldom did. She put her arm around Greta and started towing her away from the English building. "I get here a half hour early for a change, walk into the main office, and ol' meshuggener Mason comes bounding in like someone had set his shorts on fire. He rips my book bag out of my hand, grabs me by the arm, and practically drags me all the way up here. Fifty times I ask him what the hell does he think he's doing, and all he says is keep my voice down and hurry."

"It's unbelievable," Greta began.

"Shit, I'd believe anything around this place. What's the big mystery about that workroom anyway? You spill ditto fluid on some top-secret test papers or something?"

Greta was relieved Adam had picked Maxine to accompany him rather than one of the other teachers. Maxine taught art. Like Greta, she was divorced, in her early thirties, and childless. Maxine dressed like a hippie and wore far too much eye makeup. This, combined with blond frizzy hair, made Maxine, at least in appearance, the exact antithesis of Greta. She was Greta's best friend.

Greta stopped walking and turned to Maxine. "You know Belinda Jackson, don't you? She's a senior."

"Sure, I had her in Art II last semester."

"Max, she's dead. Someone killed her."

Maxine paled in spite of a generous swipe of plum blush on her cheeks. "What? You don't mean . . ." She pointed back in the direction of the workroom.

Greta nodded. "Right in there. On the floor. I found her because the door wasn't closed all the way. Her foot, the toe of her shoe, was stuck in the doorway."

"No, not Belinda. I don't believe it."

"Well, it's true."

"No wonder Mason was having fits." Maxine hugged Greta with one arm, marching her along to the administration building. "Let me get you away from here. Finding a dead student—Jesus, what a horrible way to start the day. I'll make sure I never get to work early again."

Beyond the main office, which bordered the street in front of the school, groups of students stood facing the closed gate. Two physical education teachers droned through battery-operated bullhorns, instructing the students to return to their homes. A few walked away, but most didn't budge. They simply watched the men protecting the gate from an unlikely takeover by the locked-out students. In the distance, the air filled with the shrill scream of a siren growing closer and closer.

Inside, the main office simmered with activity. Teachers, weighed down with briefcases, armloads of student papers, and the morning mail, bunched together near a makeshift sign that had been scratched in large letters on a portable chalkboard. It said: "Pupil Free Day. Teachers to remain in main office for further instructions."

The teachers seemed to know the situation was serious. When they spotted Greta and Maxine, a few members of the huddle broke loose and approached them, but Maxine warned them away with one sweeping wave of a bracelet-bejangled arm. She piloted Greta through the growing crowd and into the principal's private office.

Maxine said, "They can hardly stand it, not knowing what's going on. Did you see the look on Cecelia Hartman's face? The old gal looked like she had just given birth to teenage triplets."

"I'm glad we didn't stop to tell them the truth."

"Want me to get you something?" Maxine asked. "Coffee? Something cold? You're white as a sheet."

"No, thanks. I'll be okay." Greta sat in one of the fake leather chairs next to the principal's desk. Maxine let out a deep breath and plopped into the swivel chair behind the bulky mahogany desk.

"Grets, how about an aspirin? Maybe I should get you an aspirin?"

Grets. She'd never had a nickname as a kid, and now at thirty-three Maxine had nicknamed her Grets. Well, why not? Greta had automatically shortened Maxine to Max. Max and Grets. It sounded like a trained dog act, but the friendship had sustained Greta through the fallout from her ruined marriage. She was lucky to have such a friend.

"No aspirin. Maybe later."

"What next?" Maxine asked.

Greta shook her head. "We wait, I guess. Somebody has to tell Mrs. Jackson."

Maxine's eyes widened. "You're not going to be the one, are you? Wait. Let Adam or the police do it."

"I feel awful about dumping this in his lap, I mean after what he went through this summer with his wife."

"He's the boss, remember? That's why he gets forty grand a year more than we do."

"I know, but—"

"As your union rep, I order you to stop feeling sorry for management. The fact that his wife died has nothing to do with his job. He's getting paid plenty to shoulder this kind of responsibility. You're not."

Perhaps Maxine was right. Greta wasn't sure about where the responsibility should fall, but she did feel Adam had suffered enough grief recently. Greta, along with most of the other teachers on the staff, had attended his wife's funeral just four months ago.

Greta had never met Adam's wife, but she had wept nonetheless, saddened by the mountains of flowers and the beautifully clear day that Helen Mason never got to see. When the mourners had left the gravesite and walked back to the dozens of parked cars lining the road, Greta heard whispers about how the principal and his wife had been extremely close, and now, without even the comfort of children, Adam was all alone.

On the first day of school back in August, the teachers had found an open letter from Adam in their mailboxes. He thanked everyone for their outpouring of concern and explained how much all the cards and flowers had comforted him. Then he said McCormick High was all he had left, and the staff was now his family. A bit corny maybe, as Maxine had pointed out, but Greta still had the letter tucked away in one of her desk drawers.

The noise in the outer office grew louder. Footsteps. Then Adam opened the door. He raised one eyebrow, just slightly, in Maxine's direction, then took the chair next to Greta.

"How do you feel?"

"Okay. Stunned, I guess. I was pretty shook up when I found her, but I'll be all right."

Adam turned to Maxine. "Maxine, why don't you pick some people to handle the phones. As soon as the kids start showing up at home, parents are going to want to know what happened."

Maxine shrugged. "Okay. So what do you want us to tell them?"

Adam stood up. Most women would find him very attractive. The determined look in his eyes and his erect posture reminded Greta of a character played by Nick Nolte in a movie she had just seen on TV a few nights ago.

"The truth, of course," he said to Maxine. "The police are going to have to run tests, which could take days, but according to the homicide detectives I just talked to, it looks like the girl was strangled."

"Holy shit." Maxine went to the door, stopped, and turned back to Greta. "I'll see you later, okay?"

Greta nodded as the door closed behind Maxine. "You're asking union people to talk to the parents?"

Adam gave her a half smile. "At least they'll have something to do besides pick on me. You understand this will be a big mess for the district, don't you? We're going to hear all kinds of talk about the schools being unsafe. I'll be nailed for not having enough security."

"But this must have happened last night, after cheerleading practice. Probably after security left for the day. Belinda's mother said she never came home."

"Then you talked to her mother?" Adam asked.

"Not since I found Belinda. She called before seven to report her daughter missing, and I called back to tell her I'd let her know if the girl showed up for first period. Somebody has to call her, tell her what happened."

"I think you'd better let the police be the first to talk to her. We can both stop at her home later this afternoon if you feel up to it."

Greta met Adam's eyes. "Thanks. I'd like it if you went with me."

"Sure, I'd be glad to." He put his hand on her arm. "If you're sure you're all right, I have to give some assignments to the staff and get ready for the press. This isn't going to be an easy day for any of us."

Greta wanted to smile, but her facial muscles wouldn't respond. At the moment the word *easy* no longer seemed a part of her vocabulary.

3

GRETA avoided the teachers still huddled in the main office and in little clusters up and down the corridor and slipped into the women's rest room across the hall. She splashed cold water on her face and gazed at herself in the mirror. Her face was the color of oatmeal. Her usually clear blue eyes looked murky, somewhat like the dreary greenish blue of the rest room walls. She dried her hands on a pulpy paper towel and patted the skin under her eyes.

Adam had informed Greta that the detectives wanted to talk to her. She hoped she wouldn't fall apart when she had to tell them the details about finding Belinda. Talking about it would be like going through it all over again.

What kind of sick bastard would do such a thing? She envisioned Belinda struggling for her life with a madman, crying, begging him to stop. Why would anyone want to take the life of a sweet seventeen-year-old? Why Belinda?

She pushed the rest room door open and stepped back into the corridor. Teachers milled about, some speaking with a great deal of authority to uniformed police officers, others clucking among themselves. Maxine and at least ten other teachers who were most active in the union were missing from the group. Obviously they had scattered throughout the building, manning the phones as Adam had instructed.

"Greta," a voice called from behind, "I just heard."

She turned and faced Stanley Deep. Behind his back, Maxine and Greta jokingly called Stanley the campus stud. A marriage of twenty-plus years hadn't prevented him from making a pass at every female on the staff under the age of sixty, except maybe Vera and Cecelia Hartman. With sandy though thinning hair and deep blue eyes, he wasn't unattractive, but Greta thought he had the look of a turtle with its neck outstretched in search of food. The turtle image amused Greta to the point that Stanley's licentious behavior didn't pose a real threat. In fact, she even liked Stanley when she wasn't feeling sorry for him. It was no secret that every female Stanley tried to woo turned him down flat.

"Oh, Stanley," Greta said, "it's dreadful, isn't it?"

He nodded. "You don't expect this kind of thing to happen so close to home. Belinda was my best student in period one, a real sharp mind. That one was going places."

Algebra II, period one, room 26. Of course. Greta would have checked Stanley's classroom during period one if Belinda hadn't . . . Greta had been thinking, if Belinda hadn't turned up—but then Belinda hadn't exactly made an appearance on her own.

Stanley said, "The boss said the detectives want to talk to all her teachers."

Greta nodded in Stanley's direction. "Right, the police want to talk to her teachers and me, and I believe they're waiting for me now. I'd better go."

Stanley touched her arm lightly, as if to delay her. "Greta."

"What is it, Stanley?"

Stanley's hand fell from her wrist. "Nothing. Just good luck in there."

"Thanks."

She left Stanley and headed for the conference room adjacent to Adam's office. The architects who designed McCormick

High probably imagined that the conference room, the largest room in the administration building, would be used for small meetings, but years ago the swelling school population had made it necessary to transform the room into something more functional. An old mimeograph machine sat in one corner, and a Xerox copier, which the teachers couldn't use unless they supplied their own paper, occupied another. The massive conference table, worn smooth of its original finish, still filled the center of the room.

Adam sat at the head of the table looking somber, but his expression underwent a transformation as soon as he noticed Greta in the doorway.

"Greta," he said, standing, "are you sure you're feeling up to this?"

Greta walked all the way into the room. "Yes, I believe so."

Adam gestured toward the man standing directly behind him. "This is Detective Nick Pontrelli. He's in charge of the investigation."

Pontrelli stood near the copier. Of medium height, with dark hair and eyes, he looked about fifty and kind of beat up, as if he'd taken a couple of hard raps across the bridge of his nose. Pontrelli also looked like he didn't waste a whole lot of time smiling.

Greta offered her hand, which he shook without saying anything. He motioned with his head for Greta to sit. She took the chair next to Adam.

On the opposite wall was a door that led to Adam's private office, which was sandwiched between the conference room and the main office. The door opened and a dark-haired young woman stuck her head in.

"Nick, we got the girl's mother out here. I think you'd better see her. She walked over to the school to find out what happened—and she won't wait another minute."

Pontrelli tucked a small notebook into his pocket. "Yeah, bring her in."

Mrs. Jackson followed the woman through Adam's office into the conference room. Looking so stiff she appeared frozen, Mrs. Jackson glanced from face to face, her puffy red eyes finally settling on Greta.

"It's my baby, isn't it? What's happened to my Belinda?"

Greta moved to the fragile-looking woman and put her arms around her, unable to speak.

Mrs. Jackson began to cry, tears dripping off the edge of her chin and soaking into her shapeless blue cotton sweater.

"I knew something happened to her. She always came right home from school, always."

Pontrelli took Mrs. Jackson by the arm and led her toward the window, whispering to her just low enough so Greta couldn't catch his words. His voice was grainy, but not abrupt. He was probably used to delivering news like this.

Fumes from the duplicating fluid in the nearby mimeograph machine suddenly bothered Greta. She coughed. Usually she didn't even notice the noxious odor. Today it made her head ache.

Mrs. Jackson twisted what was left of a tissue as Pontrelli spoke. She let out a moan, sobbed, and kept saying "My poor baby" over and over.

Finally, Pontrelli turned and guided Mrs. Jackson back toward the conference table. The small, dark-haired woman rushed over and took Mrs. Jackson by the elbow.

Pontrelli said, "This is Detective Alice Zamora." He paused, then added almost reluctantly, "My partner."

Adam approached Mrs. Jackson. "I am so sorry, Mrs. Jackson. I can't imagine anything more dreadful."

She simply looked at him.

"Did you walk over here?"

Mrs. Jackson sniffled and nodded. "I saw Belinda's friends walking home. They said they didn't know why school had been canceled, but I knew."

"I'll find someone to drive you home, Mrs. Jackson," Adam said.

"I want to see my baby. Where is she?"

"Zamora, take care of her," Pontrelli said.

Detective Zamora looked frustrated. She put her hand on the doorknob, but Adam stepped over to the door.

"Let me take care of Mrs. Jackson, please," he said. "I have nothing more to add to what I've already told you, and this is more important."

Zamora glanced toward Pontrelli, apparently seeking his approval, and on his slight nod she dropped her hand from Mrs. Jackson's arm. Zamora seemed jumpy, a regular bundle of nerves, like someone who needed a cigarette in the worst way. Greta was glad the district had banned smoking in all school buildings. This one probably chain-smoked.

"When will Mrs. Jackson be able to see her daughter?" Adam asked Pontrelli.

"I think the coroner's van is still here, but it might be better if she went downtown to identify her. More privacy."

"I want to see her now," Mrs. Jackson said.

"Okay. Just the tell the driver who she is," Pontrelli said to Adam. "Tell him I said it's okay."

Now visibly wobbly, Mrs. Jackson leaned on Adam when he escorted her through the door. Pontrelli sat down next to Greta. Detective Zamora stood on the other side of the table.

Greta heard loud voices outside, one louder than the others, issuing orders. Through the window she spotted a van with ACTION NEWS stenciled on the side. Channel 2 was here already—reporters from the other TV stations wouldn't be far behind. The Channel 2 van jockeyed for a place in the visitors' parking lot in front of the school, but several police cars parked on the diagonal blocked the way, making it difficult for the TV crew to unload their cameras and equipment. Though the police officers themselves stood away from their vehicles facing the onlookers, static-laced voices squawked over their radios. Red and blue lights revolved on the rooftops of the squad cars, the eerie colors bouncing off the windowpane and reflecting onto the far wall of the conference room.

Pontrelli cleared his throat. "What do you have so far?"

Zamora opened a notebook and flipped through a few pages. "Belinda Jackson, senior, good student. No gang affiliations on the records."

"Belinda had nothing to do with gangs," Greta said. "She was a good kid; she would have gone off to college next year. She wanted to go to med school."

Pontrelli jerked his head toward Greta as if he'd forgotten she was in the room. He glanced at his notebook before he spoke. "You're Mrs. Gallagher, the girl's counselor, right? You found her."

Greta nodded. "I knew Belinda. She was a good kid."

"So you said. Forgive me, Mrs. Gallagher, but when things like this happen, the parents and teachers are always shocked. They never have any idea what these kids are into until it's too late." He turned to Zamora. "Have someone check out the gang angle."

Heat surged into Greta's face and she wiped the palms of her hands down the front of her skirt. The blood pounding through the veins in her temples wasn't doing a whole lot for her headache. "Excuse me, Detective Pontrelli, but don't we read in the papers every day about homicidal maniacs, crazed killers, who do this sort of thing just for the fun of it?"

"That stuff makes the headlines, but most of the homicides we deal with are perpetrated by someone who knew the victim, or in the case of kids like this, a gang member who had a beef with the girl or her brother or her boyfriend. Of course, the punks who run in gangs usually do their dirty work with guns or knives. Strangulation isn't their usual style."

Just then the passing bell clanged, and Greta jumped as if she wasn't used to the automatic bell system that ordered teachers and students alike to begin or end a class, even when they should eat lunch or go home.

"But we don't have a gang problem here, at least not a serious one," Greta said.

Pontrelli chuckled. "We got gang problems everywhere in this city. Even the places that don't think they got problems, got problems."

"Don't you think it could be one of those sex offenders we read about?" Greta asked.

"Sure, anything's possible, but we have gang violence coming down in places you'd never even think of. We know it's gangs. We can't always get enough hard evidence for a conviction, but we usually can pinpoint the killer. Just like you know which kids will do their homework and which ones won't."

"Maybe you've got gangs involved in your other cases, but not in Belinda's," Greta insisted.

Pontrelli clicked the point on his plastic ballpoint pen and took a long, hard look at Greta. Maybe he was trying to decide whether she had even an ounce of sense in her head. "You may be right," he said. "Tell me about her friends, especially her boyfriends."

"Don't you want to hear how I found her?"

"Sure we do." Pontrelli folded his arms across his chest and waited.

Greta told them how she had noticed the door to the English teachers' workroom was ajar. How her blood had run cold when she discovered the body.

"You touch anything?" Pontrelli asked.

Greta hesitated. "Well, I touched the light switch, the telephone, the doorknob, and of course, Belinda."

"Why 'of course'?" he asked.

"I don't know. I couldn't stand her staring at me like that, so I closed her eyes, and I touched her cheek, but just lightly."

Pontrelli made notes; so did Zamora. In fact, Zamora had written enough for a gothic novel by now, but she kept on scribbling. Pontrelli jotted down only a few words every now and then, as if through the years he had learned how to ferret out the important stuff.

Pontrelli said, "Okay, you found her dead. Now, about her boyfriends."

"Well, as far as I know, her only boyfriend over the past year has been T.P. Bench."

"The kid's name is T.P.?" Pontrelli asked.

"That's what everyone calls him. His real name is something like Thaddeus Patrick Bench . . . the third."

"Tell me about him."

Greta thought for a moment. "He's a senior, a great kid, like Belinda. Pretty good student, not straight A's if I recall, but pretty good."

Pontrelli looked up at Detective Zamora. "Get him," he said. Back to Greta. "Now, who are Mr. T.P. Bench's best friends?"

"He usually hangs around with Danny Walker. And I see him with Juan Ballestero a lot, but he's the kind of kid who has a lot of friends. Everybody likes him. Everybody liked Belinda, too."

"One person didn't like her." He turned to Zamora. "Get Walker and Ballestero."

As Zamora hurried out of the room, Greta experienced a sinking sensation. Pontrelli was going to grill these innocent kids while the real killer, the madman, got away. Sure, McCormick High had its share of vandalism, fights, petty thievery, and even an increasing problem with drugs, but not all of the kids were into criminal activity. Maybe McCormick's student body as a whole wasn't the greatest academically, but a few bright stars always emerged in every class, a few exceptional students like Belinda and T.P.

The door opened. Zamora stuck her head back in. "Bench was right outside, waiting."

Greta thought Detective Zamora looked awfully young to be so matter-of-fact and hard-nosed about her job. Was that a requirement for her position or just something she'd learned from Pontrelli?

"Good," Pontrelli said. "Bring him in."

She looked surprised. "You want to talk to him now?"

"Yeah. Mr. Mason asked if we could have a staff member present when we interviewed kids. He's worried about legalities, school district red tape." He turned to Greta. "You don't mind sitting in on this, do you?"

"No, not at all," she answered, but she wasn't certain she wanted to watch Pontrelli in action. She tried to think of a way to back out gracefully, but the door opened and T.P. followed Detective Zamora into the room.

T.P. Bench looked like a choirboy in his black pullover sweater with the collar of a white shirt carefully folded over the neck. He was tall, but not as gangly as many boys his age, and his skin was remarkably clear. His dark brown eyes darted from Pontrelli to Greta.

"Everybody's talking, Ms. Gallagher. About Belinda. Is it true?" T.P. asked.

"I'm so sorry," she whispered.

"Sit down, son. Tell me your full name, so we can get it right," Pontrelli said, almost gently.

The boy's eyes swelled with tears. "T.P. Bench."

"Your *full* name, please."

"Thaddeus Patrick Bench . . . the third," he said, suffering with every syllable. T.P. looked at Pontrelli. "What happened to Belinda? Please tell me."

"Well, son," Pontrelli began slowly, "that's what we're trying to piece together. Why don't we start with you telling us about the last time you saw her. You did see her yesterday after school, didn't you?"

"Yeah, I waited for her; she had cheerleading practice. I studied in the library for a while, then I walked over to the gym and waited until she was finished."

Pontrelli looked to Greta. "The gym. That's—"

"Right across the service drive from the English building where I found her."

Pontrelli nodded and made a note. "Then what happened when cheerleading practice was over?"

T.P. began to cry. He didn't make any sounds, but tears trickled down his cheeks. "We went for a walk. Belinda said she wanted to talk."

Pontrelli leaned closer. "And what did you talk about?"

The boy looked more miserable every second. He wiped his nose with the back of his hand. "She started talking about her senior year being too important to waste going out on dates. She was sick of the way us kids raised hell—excuse me," he said to Greta. "I mean, she was sick of wasting her time with parties and stuff."

"Belinda was sick of parties?"

"Well, something like that. She just decided she had to spend more time studying, so she could get top grades. After college, she was going to try for medical school."

"So, her family could afford medical school?" Pontrelli asked.

"No, she was counting on a scholarship, maybe combined with a grant. She was pretty sure she wouldn't have a problem."

Pontrelli raised his shoulders, and his stubby neck suddenly became even shorter. "How could she be certain she'd receive a scholarship?" He looked to Greta. "They know about scholarships already?"

T.P. answered for Greta. "Well, she wasn't really certain. We don't find out for sure until next spring, but Belinda didn't think she'd have any trouble getting the money she needed."

"So what did all of this have to do with you?"

"Belinda wanted to be a doctor real bad. She said being tied down to a steady boyfriend this year would get in the way of her goals."

"That meant you. She didn't want to be tied down by you, is that it?" Pontrelli looked positively victorious.

More tears gushed from T.P.'s eyes. "Yeah. Just like that, she said she didn't want to go steady with me anymore. No matter how much I begged her not to, Belinda broke up with me."

4

PONTRELLI played with T.P. like a cat plays with a dying mouse. He spoke gently enough, at first, and sucked the kid in with his steady, almost fatherly tone. "So I guess you hated Belinda for breaking up with you like that?"

T.P. looked wounded, but he didn't come apart the way some kids would have. "No, I didn't hate her. I loved her. I'll always love her."

"How many times did you two have sex?"

T.P. winced noticeably. He hesitated. "Well . . . it wasn't . . ."

"Speak up, boy." Pontrelli pounced on him. "I asked you a question."

Greta bolted to her feet, her chair almost toppling over behind her. T.P. flashed a pained look in her direction.

"Listen," Greta said, "if you're going to grill the kid on every detail of his personal life, maybe I'd better leave. You can have the principal sit in on this line of questioning."

Greta's molars ached from the way she clenched her teeth, and she finally understood why Pontrelli was getting to her. Pontrelli's perverse skill of nailing home his point no matter whose feelings were crushed was an unwanted reminder of her ex-husband, Carl. Jesus, she hated the way memories of their verbal battlefield could spring to life when she least expected it, especially after she'd worked so hard to forget the four caustic years of her marriage.

"Okay," Pontrelli said, one side of his mouth curling into a sneer. "I can wait on the answer to that for now. What happened next?"

Greta sat down again and tried deep, measured breaths, like she had once learned in a yoga class.

T.P. studied his fingernails as if he had just discovered they were growing there on the ends of his fingers. "She walked along with me to the front gate, then she remembered she needed a book from her locker. I wanted to walk back with her, but she said no. She went to her locker, I guess, and I went home. I called her last night, four times, but her mom said she never came home." His voice faded to a whisper. He sounded tired, his words slow and furry.

"What time did you get home?"

"I dunno. I walked slow. I guess it was after five."

"You guess. Was it or wasn't it after five?"

"Right about five."

"Who was there?"

"Nobody. My parents had to meet some people—in Santa Monica, I think—so they went right from work."

Pontrelli wrote that down. "What time did your parents get home?"

T.P. shrugged. "Ten or ten-thirty, I guess."

"So from five to ten or ten-thirty, you were completely alone?"

T.P. nodded without taking his eyes away from his fingertips.

"You see anyone? You talk to anyone—on the phone, maybe?"

T.P. shook his head.

"You got no one to verify any of this?"

"I was alone. I can't prove where I was, but I swear I didn't kill Belinda."

Pontrelli stood up, ignoring T.P.'s last statement. "Okay, kid, that's all for now."

T.P. shuffled out of the conference room. Greta couldn't remember ever seeing him shuffle before.

Pontrelli looked at his notes. "I have five teachers to talk to, see if they know anything, and I also want to speak to the custodians who may have been around after four."

"I'll be in the counseling office if you need me," Greta said, now feeling even more reluctant about sitting in on Pontrelli's student interviews. On second thought, however, maybe she could prevent Pontrelli from using his strong-arm tactics on the kids. Yeah, just about the same way she could stop a DC-10 with a silk scarf.

The main office was still buzzing. Stanley Deep stood with Maxine along the wall near the dozens of small wooden pigeon-hole compartments that served as the teachers' mailboxes. He grinned when he saw Greta.

"You were with them a long time," he said.

"They have any clues yet?" Maxine asked.

"I don't know about clues," Greta answered. "Detective Pontrelli just gave T.P. Bench the third degree. He was pretty rough on him."

"A kid like T.P. wouldn't resort to violence; not his style," Stanley said.

Greta and Maxine both looked at him in surprise.

"Since when have you ever noticed anything about any of the boys in your classes?" Maxine asked. "We thought you didn't even know they were in the room."

"I don't know what you're talking about," Stanley answered, his lower lip drooping somewhat. "You have to look at this objectively, and T.P.'s not their man."

"So who is?" Greta asked.

Stanley's eyes darted around the room before he spoke. "Just between us, of course, if I were the cops, I'd check out Juan Ballestero. I've seen him sniffing around Belinda in math class."

"Get serious," Maxine said. "Juan's not the violent type either. Hell, when he was in my art class last year, all he wanted to paint was animal rights posters."

"No kidding?" Stanley said. "Now that I think of it, it's hard to picture any of the kids in my Algebra II as killers, and all of Belinda's friends are in that class."

Greta said, "Why does everyone think it had to be one of the kids? What about a psycho, a maniac? Why's that so hard to believe?"

Stanley said, "That's not hard to believe at all, especially nowadays."

"Thanks," Greta said. "I'm glad there's at least one other person who agrees with me."

Stanley propped his arm against one of the mailboxes, pinning Greta and Maxine in the corner. "Listen, when we're finished here for the day, why don't the three of us go out for a drink?"

"Stanley, why don't you get a life?" Maxine said, ducking under his outstretched arm. "Better yet, go home and have a drink with your wife." Stanley quickly lowered his hand.

Greta grabbed Maxine's arm and yanked her toward the door. "We'll see you later, Stanley," Greta called back to him. "We have to man the phones."

When they were out of earshot, Greta released her grip on Maxine. "You didn't have to shoot him down that hard. He's harmless."

"He's a schmuck."

"Well, sure, but offering to buy us a drink isn't exactly an invitation to bed us down for the night."

"What night? With him, it would be minutes. No, probably seconds."

Greta laughed. "You really know how to hurt a guy."

They walked into the counseling office and headed for Greta's private office. The phone was ringing.

"I'll get it," Maxine said. "The front office is transferring all calls to the counselors' phones. I've already talked to about nine million parents."

Maxine ran ahead of Greta but stopped short when she almost collided with Rudy Smith, one of the school's custodians, who was just leaving Greta's private office.

"Just checking the locks on all the doors," Rudy said without meeting Greta's eyes. "Thought I'd start in the offices."

Greta thought he sounded too eager to explain. Like a kid who had done his homework for the first time all semester. "Why?" she asked. "The lock on my office hasn't worked for the last three years. I've sent you a request to repair it about fifty times."

Rudy squinted his already foxlike eyes into narrow black slits. Short and wiry, Rudy was probably in his mid-twenties. He rattled a giant ring holding what looked like a hundred keys; his hands looked dirty from some kind of grease.

Of all the custodians on the staff, Rudy was the least likable. He skulked about, pretending to sweep, when it was obvious the broom was little more than a prop. Greta pegged him as lazy, but what really bothered her was the way Rudy watched the girls, perhaps jangling his ring of keys to get their attention, even when he was supposedly working. Not that he'd ever been reported for improper conduct, but Greta wouldn't put it past him. She didn't like Rudy, and she especially didn't like him poking around her office.

"Yeah," Rudy said, wiping the back of his hand across his mouth. "We got all your requests, but we also got a whole school to run. They just cut us back again, so between the day shift and the night man, we've got only five people doing everything around here. It ain't easy in a school this size."

Greta focused on the flakes of dandruff sprinkled over the shoulders of Rudy's denim shirt. Even his dry scalp annoyed her. "Well, is it fixed now?"

"Huh? Oh, the lock. No, I need to replace it altogether." With that, Rudy disappeared into Fran Elliot's office next door.

Greta went inside her cubicle and closed the door. Maxine hung up the phone.

"What was that all about?" Maxine asked.

"Rudy said he was checking the locks." Greta glanced at the miscellaneous notes and memos strewn across her desk. She hated a messy desk, but somehow whenever she took care of one pile of paperwork, three more sprang up to take its place. On top of her stack of notes regarding tardies, she spotted Belinda's program card. She had forgotten to return it to the file box. A tiny black smudge glistened on the upper right-hand corner of the card. She examined it closely.

"Max, Rudy touched this. Look." She thrust the card in front of Maxine for a second, then pulled it back and studied it again. "I saw his hands. His fingers were greasy."

Maxine stared at her. "What do you think he was looking for?"

"I don't know."

"Maybe you should tell Dick Tracy or whatever his name is," Maxine said. "Rudy has no business messing with the files on your desk, especially files that concerned Belinda."

Greta sat down. "I don't think he'll listen. Pontrelli is bent on hanging this on one of Belinda's friends unless he can turn it into a gang war. He said the killer was probably someone Belinda knew."

"So? Rudy probably knew Belinda. He's here on campus every day, isn't he? Tell Pontrelli."

"Yeah, I guess I should," Greta answered, but something told her Pontrelli would fall down laughing if she presented him with a clue, especially one as vague as a grease smudge on a program card. He would probably consider her an overgrown Nancy Drew who should let the police do their jobs without interference from amateurs.

The phone rang; Maxine grabbed it. She spoke for a second, then hung up. "That was Dick Tracy's sidekick. She said Pontrelli wants you in the conference room ASAP. He's got Juan Ballestero in leg irons and the kid is ready to talk."

5

PONTRELLI occupied the same chair in the conference room; Juan Ballestero sat on his right. From this angle Greta saw that Pontrelli's face sagged into tired lines. He also needed a haircut. A Styrofoam cup half full of black coffee sat near Pontrelli's right hand.

The room was stuffy, still heavy with fumes from the duplicating fluid, and now the air had grown stagnant from having the doors shut all day. Greta thought about opening a window but decided Pontrelli would not be interested in waiting around while she tended to housekeeping. She sat down on the other side of Juan.

Juan was a long stringy kid with underdeveloped shoulders, but his even white teeth and a mane of magnificent black hair pretty much overshadowed his skinny physique.

"It's true what they're saying about Belinda, isn't it, Ms. Gallagher? Why won't he tell me anything?" Juan asked, jerking his head toward Pontrelli.

"He was waiting for me, I believe," she answered.

Pontrelli didn't wait for Greta to explain further. "Belinda Jackson, a friend of yours, I believe, was murdered last night."

Juan went completely white. He looked at Greta. She nodded.

Juan said, "I didn't believe it at first, but then when T.P.

wouldn't stop to talk to me a little while ago . . . Jesus, poor Belinda. She was such a nice kid."

Pontrelli went into action. "I guess a lot of the boys would be interested in a nice-looking girl like Belinda. And those short little cheerleading skirts get the guys all revved up, don't they?"

Juan looked confused, but he nodded and raised his shoulders in a halfhearted shrug.

"You ever take her out?" Pontrelli asked.

"Yeah, one time back in tenth grade we went to a dance. We had a great time."

"So what happened? She dump you for this Bench kid, or what?"

Juan flushed and lowered his eyes. "My mom said I couldn't go to any more dances or date anyone until I pulled up my grades in biology."

Pontrelli looked like someone had just splashed a bucket of cold water in his face. He coughed.

"Detective Pontrelli," Greta said, "these kids aren't as deeply involved in dangerous liaisons as you might think."

Pontrelli frowned but otherwise ignored her comment. "So forget about the dance in tenth grade. Tell me about the last time you talked to the girl."

Juan ran his fingers through his hair. "Yesterday I saw her in first period, Algebra. I asked her something about the homework assignment, that's all."

"Did you set up a meeting with her? A date maybe?"

"No."

"You didn't know she was planning to break up with her boyfriend?"

"Yeah, I knew, but she didn't tell me yesterday."

Pontrelli looked at Juan, fighting a little smile on the left side of his mouth. "So, you knew about her plan all along."

Juan squirmed in his chair. "About a week or two ago she told me she might break off with T.P."

"She just happened to mention this, out of the blue?"

"Sort of."

"That interest you, knowing she would be available?" Pontrelli spoke slowly, like a teacher does in order to make a point very clear.

"Belinda and me, well, we were just good friends. I liked her a lot, but I've been going out with Irene since last summer. Irene Flores. You know her, don't you, Ms. Gallagher?"

Greta knew Irene, another one of her counselees. Nice girl. Belinda's best friend, as far as Greta knew.

"Okay," Pontrelli said, "so what happened yesterday after math class? You saw her later in the day, didn't you? Maybe at lunch or after school?"

Juan thought for a moment. "Hey, I think I did see Belinda at lunch, but I didn't talk to her. She was way over next to the hash lines, talking to the principal."

"Did you talk to her after school?" Pontrelli asked. "Maybe you tried to cheer her up about her broken romance?"

"No, I went over to Irene's. We studied for a while, then we went to pick up Irene's little brother at her aunt's house."

"The aunt can verify this?"

"Yes."

Pontrelli coughed into his hand. "All right. I'll probably need to talk to you again. See that Detective Zamora has your home address and make sure you come to school on Monday, you hear?"

Juan shrugged, this time more convincingly. "Sure, why wouldn't I?"

Pontrelli opened the door for Juan. Adam stood right outside the conference room, waiting. Rudy Smith and one of the other custodians, a tall, slender middle-aged fellow, stood with him. Greta followed Juan out of the room, passing close to Rudy. As Rudy shifted his weight from one foot to the other, his eyes seemed to darken, penetrating her own, as if he knew she had discovered the grease smudge.

"Excuse me." She turned to Pontrelli. "Could I talk to you privately for just a second before you start your next round of questioning?"

Pontrelli stared at her. "I'll be right with you," he said casually to Adam and the two custodians. He closed the door and waited for Greta to speak.

"This may not mean anything," she began, "but I thought you should know."

"Yeah?" Pontrelli said.

Greta's fingernails bit into her palms, and she quickly relaxed her tightened fists. "Earlier, I guess while you were talking to Belinda's teachers, one of the custodians waiting outside, the little guy, Rudy Smith, went into my office. He touched a card on my desk that had personal information about Belinda written on it. Her address, telephone number, that kind of thing."

"He touched the card? That's all?"

"Well, he acted a little jumpy when I caught him leaving my office."

A glimmer, maybe just the beginning of a smirk, crossed Pontrelli's face, then stopped. "Okay, I'll check him out."

Greta clenched her teeth. She wasn't imagining it. Dealing with Pontrelli was like dickering with Carl all over again. She was certain he wouldn't check out Rudy, if only because she had suggested it.

"Thanks," she said. "I just thought you should know."

She hurried out of the room past Rudy and the other custodian. Adam stopped her in the doorway leading to the main hallway. "How are you doing?" he asked.

Greta wanted to scream. She felt like a child who had just tattled to the teacher and then been scolded for doing so. Pontrelli had thought her information was useless. She certainly wasn't going to make the mistake of repeating it to Adam.

Adam waited, a concerned look on his face, while Greta composed herself. "I'm okay."

"I've sent most of the teachers home. The parents will get the full story on the five o'clock news, and Pontrelli should be finished with you for the day. We can leave whenever you'd like to pay our respects to Mrs. Jackson."

"Let me help Maxine with the phone calls for a couple of hours. Why don't we leave here about four? By then I'll need a break."

Adam smiled as if he understood. "Would you like to go in one car?"

"No, I'll take my car so I don't get locked in. I'm parked over by the bungalows."

"You have Belinda's address?" he asked.

"Yes, I've been to the house."

"Okay, I'll meet you there about four."

Greta and Maxine took turns fielding phone calls until after three. Greta finally got up from her desk, arching her stiff back in a stretch.

"You gonna be all right?" Maxine asked.

"Sure. I'm kinda numb from the neck up, but all my other parts seem to be working."

"You could visit Mrs. Jackson tomorrow."

"I'd rather go now. She probably needs to be surrounded by lots of people."

Maxine paused in the doorway for a moment. "I'll talk to you later, okay?"

"Okay, and thanks for everything, Max."

Greta retrieved her purse from her file cabinet in the counseling office. On her way out she inspected the lock on her office door and the surrounding paint. No signs of grease. Rudy hadn't touched it.

The walk across the empty campus seemed longer than usual. Even the reporters with their electronic gadgetry had gone. Greta regretted she had chosen a safe place to park her car rather than the faculty lot closer to the offices. A few years ago, when a jump in student population forced the addition of the two portable buildings, the surrounding earth had been layered over with several coatings of blacktop. The first twenty or so teachers to arrive each day squeezed their cars between the bungalows, hoping the close proximity of two watchful teachers would prevent the vandalism that plagued the more defenseless cars in the main faculty lot.

She slowed as she approached the English building. Bright yellow bands of plastic cordoned off the teachers' workroom and the concrete just outside the door: POLICE LINE DO NOT CROSS. She picked up her pace.

The day had warmed, as Greta knew it would, but now it was growing cool again. The sun disappeared behind a cloud. She hated to see the days grow shorter as they did this time of year. In the fading light, McCormick High looked especially run-down. The school's exterior hadn't been properly painted in years, even though work crews had painted over some of the more elaborate graffiti. Their efforts, in colors never quite matching the faded stucco, had left the school with mottled walls that looked almost diseased.

Somewhere, in the distance, she heard a metal trash can scraping against concrete. One of the custodians, maybe Rudy, was sweeping somewhere. She raised up on her toes to muffle the sound of her footsteps.

6

GRETA got into her car, relocked the door on the driver's side, and started the engine. A chill crept beneath her skin, and her shoulders gave a little involuntary shudder.

She drove the short distance to Mrs. Jackson's house, passing the familiar vacant lots and run-down apartment buildings without really noticing them. When she pulled over and parked, she was relieved to see Adam standing on the sidewalk waiting for her.

They visited with Mrs. Jackson for over an hour. Friends dropped by, mostly women Mrs. Jackson's age, some red-faced from crying, some carrying the inevitable covered casserole dish or a hastily baked cake. With each arrival, Mrs. Jackson introduced Greta and Adam, and the hushed voices of the visitors grew louder, curious about the grisly details of the murder but mindful of respect for the grieving mother. Greta let Adam do most of the talking, and when Belinda's twenty-year-old brother arrived home from college looking dazed and exhausted, they took the opportunity to say their good-byes.

Greta breathed easier when they reached the sidewalk. "Nothing we say can really help Mrs. Jackson. It's so incredibly sad."

"I don't know," Adam answered. "When Helen died, the words didn't matter, but the fact that people came over, that they cared ..." He turned away from her and activated a beeper, unlocking his car door.

"Well, then I'm glad we went. I just felt so useless."

Adam looked at her, his bold, square jawline silhouetted against the gray evening sky. "Don't ever think what you say is useless. Mrs. Jackson hung on your every word, just like the kids do at school. I don't know how you do it."

Greta searched his eyes. She had always thought Adam considered her just one of the staff, another name on the payroll.

"I don't know about you," Adam said, "but I'm starting to regret I missed lunch. Can I interest you in dinner?"

A sudden increase in Greta's pulse rate surprised her. "I'm afraid I'd be lousy company tonight."

"I find that hard to believe, but lousy company is better than no company. I hate always eating alone."

She needed a swift kick. Why hadn't she picked up on Adam's obvious loneliness? She was thinking union again. Teachers and principals in their separate corners.

"Thanks," she said. "I'd love to have dinner with you. Where shall we go?"

"Pick a place close to where you live, so you won't have a long drive home."

Greta chose Maria's Kitchen. The tiny place was far too noisy and definitely not romantic, even though it was Italian. Wonderful spicy aromas filled the air. The waiter maneuvered them through cramped aisles between the tables to a postage-stamp-size table in the corner. A busboy appeared almost instantly and deposited a basket of hot buttered herb bread between them.

Adam brushed a crumb from the black-and-white check-ered oilcloth covering the table. He picked up a small wedge of bread and drew in the aroma of the fresh-cut herbs. "Um, rosemary. This smells great. I like this place already."

"They have a wonderful pasta with fresh tomatoes and

basil, just the right touch of garlic. I try to avoid red meat myself, but their meat sauce is supposed to be excellent also," Greta said. She paused, waiting for Adam to go into a protein, meat, and potatoes tirade the way some men did when she expressed her food preferences.

He didn't even flinch. "Tomato and basil sounds good. I'll try it."

Greta smiled. "You'll love the food here; everything is fresh."

Adam did love the food. He attacked, rather than ate, his salad and pasta, and Greta liked the way he behaved like a hungry teenager rather than a stuffy school administrator. Though she had worked with him for over a year, she knew almost nothing personal about him. She watched the way he held his fork and the way he tilted his head. His gestures were decidedly masculine, yet there was a certain gentleness about him that Greta liked very much. How in hell would she ever explain this act of treason to Maxine?

"So tell me," Adam said, "what do you do when you're not working miracles with McCormick's students or doing yeoman's service on our school-based management team?"

"The usual, I guess. I like to travel. I read a lot. I used to love to hike and swim in the summer, but now I mostly just putter around the house. Now that I'm finally a homeowner, I've become a regular Mrs. Fixit."

"I have a drain that keeps backing up. Maybe you could take a look at it?"

"Be glad to. Just remember I'm union—I charge union rates."

Adam laughed. "You like sports? I'm kind of a ski bum myself, and I follow the Lakers. I bet you're a football fan."

"You lose. Maxine's the football nut. I've been true blue ever since I was a kid. I grew up in Echo Park near Dodger

Stadium. My brother sold peanuts there in the summer, and he used to get me in free."

"Really? I don't run into too many female Dodger fans."

"Are you kidding? There are droves of us. We're the team's true inspiration."

"Well, I like baseball, too. Why don't we take in a couple of home games together next season? Maybe next year they'll win the pennant."

He was thinking next season. "Sounds like fun. Just don't try to get me on skis."

"It's not as hard as it looks. You'd probably pick it up in three lessons."

Greta shook her head. "You don't understand. Skiing is something you do in snow. I don't do anything in snow if I can help it."

The restaurant was quieter now that some of the other patrons had left. The remaining customers, mostly couples with their heads inclined toward one another, spoke softly. Greta heard the pulse of a slow-turning ceiling fan rotating above their heads.

After they had worked their way through dinner and wine, down to small dishes of spumoni ice cream and cups of steaming coffee, Adam said, "I'm really sorry you had to be the one to find Belinda. This is a nasty business we have to face, you know?"

"I know. I wish I felt better about the police. Why did we have to get stuck with a hard-nose like Pontrelli?"

Adam leaned back, one hand resting lightly on the rim of his coffee cup. "Pontrelli seems coarse, but I'm sure he knows what he's doing. It's important that we help him as much as possible."

"Important to whom? I don't like the way he tries to twist everything the kids say. Embarrassing our students doesn't get him any closer to the killer."

"Greta, I know you're the champion of all these kids, but it could have been one of them. Kids have been known to wipe out entire families in a moment of anger. Little things can set them off."

She pressed her napkin against her lips. The waistband on her skirt felt very tight, almost painful. "I'm sorry, I can't believe it was one of Belinda's friends. I just can't."

"Well, we know it wasn't Danny Walker. Did Pontrelli tell you?"

"No, what about Danny?" she asked, leaning closer.

"I called the homes of a whole list of boys. Pontrelli had been picking up names here and there, so he asked me to check them out for alibis. Danny came down with a bad case of the flu early yesterday morning, and according to his mother, he hasn't moved out of the bed except for two or three trips to the bathroom ever since."

"What about the other boys?"

"Most of them were in places where adults were around to verify what the kids were up to. I think T.P. is the only one who has no one to vouch for him."

"T.P. wouldn't hurt a fly," she said.

"I guess you know him better than I do."

"Look, you teach a kid, and then counsel him in everything from his reason for whacking a kid with a book when he was in the tenth grade to his choice of college as a senior, you get to know him pretty well."

Adam smiled, his blue-gray eyes twinkling ever so slightly. "I love the way you crusade. These kids don't know how lucky they are."

Greta looked away from him, focusing on the little puddle of coffee in the bowl of her spoon. "I just do my job."

"And you do it beautifully."

Greta hesitated, almost reluctant to break the spell Adam was weaving. Finally she said, "What did Belinda talk to you about at lunch yesterday?"

Adam stiffened. He straightened the napkin spread across his lap. "Belinda? I don't remember talking to Belinda yesterday."

"Juan Ballestero said he saw the two of you talking over by the hash lines."

He thought for a moment. "Wasn't that the day before? I think it was Wednesday; I'm sure of it."

"It doesn't matter, I was just wondering what was troubling Belinda."

"I talk to so many kids in the course of a week that the conversations all run together." He rubbed his chin. "I think it had something to do with homecoming. The cheerleading squad and homecoming."

Greta licked the last tiny bit of ice cream from her spoon. "That makes sense. I thought she might have needed help with a personal problem."

Adam chuckled. "Who are you trying to kid? For a real problem, she would have gone directly to you. For the stuff that has to do with protocol or to get permission for some school activity is as far as they trust me."

Greta laughed. "It's rough being a figurehead."

Adam smiled. If only he weren't so good-looking. Surely Maxine would send her union goons to tar and feather anyone who harbored the thoughts she was now thinking about a principal.

"Hey," he said, glancing at his watch, "I didn't mean to monopolize you on a Friday evening. I'm sure you have plans."

Should she pretend she was sought after by every horn-rimmed educator type in town or explain that she would be returning to an empty house? She didn't even have a dog.

"No plans," she said, "but I am tired."

Adam paid the bill and walked Greta down the block to her Toyota. The busy street hummed with traffic. Most of the shops were closed, but window displays and neon signs cast their bright colors upon the sidewalk. A reflection of pink and yellow light from the window of an antiques shop played in Adam's eyes when he gazed at a collection of old toys. Adam's hand lightly touched her elbow as they circled around an oncoming couple. It had been years since she had been part of a couple. His touch evoked memories, good memories.

"Drive safely," he said when she got into her car. "And thanks for not bringing up a lot of union gripes. Those I hear all day long."

Greta laughed. "I guess I missed my opportunity to solicit a little help with our stalled contract negotiations."

He grinned. "You overestimate my power. There isn't a damn thing I can do to salvage that mess."

"Not even a good word for a cost-of-living increase on the new contract?"

"The board doesn't care two rips about what I think. They just want their principals to run a tight ship so the kids don't get murdered on campus. I guess you already know the teachers are going to have to be more visible. Yard duty—at least for a while."

"The union won't like it. Teachers are supposed to teach. Let the board hire some cops."

"I know. And for what it's worth, I'm on your side."

"Thanks," she said, waving. "Good night."

When Greta pulled into her driveway at home, her living room windows glowed brightly, lit up like the nearby mall the week before Christmas. Good old Maxine. Greta wasn't returning to an empty house after all. Greta and Maxine had exchanged house keys for convenience shortly after Greta's divorce was initiated, and Maxine showed up, as if by some uncanny sixth sense, every time Greta needed someone to talk to. Maxine didn't believe in conserving any energy except her own, so it wouldn't do any good to remind her about wasting electricity.

The blaring lights were a part of Maxine's presence. When Greta let herself in, the stereo thumped with the ancient sounds of the Doors playing "Light My Fire." The bass echoed loudly, vibrating anything that was loose in the living room. Greta turned down the volume two levels.

The living room held only a sofa and two matching chairs (leftovers from her days with Carl), a few end tables with lamps, her stereo, and a stationary bicycle she never found time to use. One of Maxine's paintings, actually a huge relief painted over thick layers of plaster, hung majestically over the sofa. Last summer she had wallpapered the room herself, and the job could easily pass for professional.

The kitchen lights glared through the doorway. Greta heard the refrigerator door slam. Maxine, her hair frizzed in every conceivable direction, shambled into the living room carrying a bag of barbecue potato chips. She had traded her shoes for Greta's old house slippers.

Maxine said, "You're out of Diet Coke. You actually expect people to drink pomegranate juice?"

Greta kicked off her shoes and sat down. "I happen to like pomegranate juice; it's good for you."

"Tastes like Robitussin cough syrup."

"Well, it's better for you than Diet Coke, and why don't you have an apple instead of those greasy chips? I just bought some pippins. They're organic."

"So's horseshit—"

"Yeah, I know, but that doesn't mean we have to eat it." Greta threw her head back against the sofa cushion and groaned. "I give up. You are completely hopeless."

Maxine's laughter ricocheted around the room, but then a serious deliberation crept into her eyes. "Hey, Greta you been at Mrs. Jackson's all this time?"

"No, I had dinner."

Maxine took a long look at Greta. "I stopped at Burger King

for something to eat, then I came directly over here because I was sure you'd be a mess, crying your eyes out over Belinda, depressed as hell. Instead, you look like you just got laid."

Greta laughed. "Considering what an awful day this has been, I guess I do feel better than I thought I would. After we left Mrs. Jackson's, I had a chance to unwind."

"We?"

"Adam and I went to dinner. It was nice, really very pleasant."

"Shit, how could dinner with him be pleasant?"

"Max, stuff your union banner for a change, will you? He's just a man, not some druid sent by the board of education to offer us up as human sacrifices."

Maxine bit into a chip, munched it loudly, then said, "Well, I'll admit he's not as bad as some of the principals I've known, but he's still one of *them.*"

"Our beef is with the school board, not with every administrator in the district."

"This is only Adam's second year at McCormick. They never show their true colors the first year, but in another month or so he'll be assigning teachers to yard duty or some other damn thing. You'll see." Maxine raised the almost-empty chip bag to her lips and poured the few remaining crumbs into her mouth. That done, she crumpled the bag into a crackly little ball.

"If he assigns us yard duty it'll be because of security. Because of what happened to Belinda."

Maxine drew her eyebrows together, puzzled. "So where'd you go?"

"Just to Maria's. Nothing fancy."

"You make another date with him?"

"Of course not. It just so happened we were together, and we were both hungry, so we stopped for something to eat. That's it. Case closed."

The phone rang. Greta walked across the living room and grabbed it on the second ring. "Hello."

"Greta? It's me, Adam. I just wanted to make certain you made it home all right."

"Oh, yes, thank you. I'm fine."

"Good, well, good night. Oh, by the way, I really enjoyed having dinner with you tonight."

"Yes, it was a pleasant ending to a terrible day. Thank you."

"Maybe the next time we get together . . . off campus, I mean . . . it will be under happier circumstances."

"Yes, I hope so," she answered. They wished each other good-night. Greta dropped the phone into its cradle.

Maxine stared at Greta, her eyes as wide and shiny as the burnished gold hoops dangling from her ears. "Was that who I think it was?"

Greta tried to dream up a plausible lie, but since she seldom got away with lying to Maxine anyway, there was no real point in trying. "It was Adam, wondering if I made it home all right."

"You gave him your number?"

"Max, it's on the faculty roster, remember? So's yours."

"You'll become a different person if you start up with him. Principals have some sort of genetic mutation that gradually takes over the thought waves of other people. It's like mind control."

"You're full of it," Greta said.

"No, I mean it. You'll stop going to our union wine-and-cheese parties, and you'll end up socializing with retired principals. They eat hot dogs, you know."

"My being friends with Adam won't change a thing, and I suspect he likes the same kind of food I do. Tonight he ordered pasta without meat, same as me."

"He's not a vegetarian," Maxine said. "Did he tell you he was?"

"No, but when I mentioned I don't eat red meat, he ordered what I did."

Maxine smiled. "Sure, he played along and suckered you the first time. Next thing you know you'll be at one of those incredibly boring parties for administrators. When they're done trashing the union contract and thinking up new ways to make teachers suffer, they'll force you to eat little cocktail wienies off toothpicks. Case closed."

7

UNLIKE most Saturdays, this one dragged for Greta. She tried to take her mind off the murder by cleaning the house, but no matter how many windows she polished or how many dust bunnies she captured, her thoughts returned to Belinda. She washed three loads of laundry and put clean sheets on her bed. How the hell was she supposed to shake the terrible vision of the dead girl from her mind?

Saturday night Maxine had a blind date, so Greta sat home alone, grading American Lit essays. She played some old Beatles records on the stereo, softly, for background noise. Talk about a thrilling social life.

When she was a kid in high school, her mother had always chided her for sitting home on weekends with her nose in a book. God, those had been awful days. She argued with her mother about everything, even the tiniest things that didn't make a bit of difference. But the rift between them had not grown out of the little arguments. They disagreed on every topic of importance in Greta's young life, or maybe it was just that, like all teenagers, she felt so strongly about her convictions. Like the day she announced to her mother she wanted to go to college.

"College?" her mother had said without taking her eyes off

"General Hospital" on TV. "You know I can't afford to send you to college."

"I can work. I'll apply for scholarships."

"You can't work and study at the same time."

"Sure you can—lots of kids do it."

"Why don't you just get a job like your brother? He didn't need no fancy college to make good money."

"Ma, he's a construction worker! You want me to be a construction worker?"

"I never said that."

Now, of course, she understood that her mother had done her best to raise two kids by herself. Greta had been only eight and her brother thirteen when their father died in an automobile accident. Her mother had worked hard, but Greta had been too young and self-involved to appreciate her mother's sacrifices at the time. Greta went to college, waiting tables to pay her way and ignoring her mother's comments about all that money just for a couple of books. Then, when maturity finally settled in at age twenty, Greta lost her mother. A heart attack ended all the petty arguments forever.

Greta often wondered if things would be different between them today if her mother had lived. She liked to think her mother would have mellowed and would have become a real friend by now. God, this thing with Belinda was turning her into a sentimental mess.

It was still hard to believe Belinda was dead. Greta hoped Belinda hadn't waged too many wars with her mother, but if she knew anything at all about kids, she knew the chances of a teenager's seeing eye to eye with a parent were pretty slim. Belinda had even argued with T.P. about her need to have more time for her studies. And this only because she wanted to make certain she would be eligible for scholarship money. If Belinda hadn't been so headstrong, T.P. would've walked with her to her locker. The killer wouldn't have bothered the two of them. Who had been lurking in the shadows that afternoon? A madman or the familiar face of Rudy Smith?

First thing Sunday morning, Maxine phoned with the details of last night's date. "Bona fide boring," Maxine said.

"Where'd you go?"

"Would you believe we heard chamber music at the L.A. Art Museum?"

"So what's wrong with that? Wasn't the music any good?"

"Good isn't the issue. That's probably the cheapest live performance in the city."

Greta laughed. "It's the thought that counts."

Maxine moaned. "Listen, if you're so intrigued with Mr. Cheapskate, I'll give him your number. You might enjoy a big night out in a Budget Rent-a-Car."

"Thanks, but I don't need your rejects," Greta said. "I wasn't crazy about hand-me-downs even when I was a kid."

At least the phone call from Maxine improved her spirits. Then, Sunday night, Greta drove over to Maxine's place for the evening. No matter how many times Greta visited Maxine's condo, she was always overwhelmed by the barrage of colors and clutter. Nothing matched. Pillows heaped in corners were the closest things to chairs, although Maxine did have a recycled sofa in front of the TV. The throw rugs had all been loomed by hand back when Maxine had taken a weaving class in college. But the real shocker was the artwork literally covering every inch of wall space in every room—including the bathroom. Maxine created incredible three-dimensional relief paintings that took on the quality of sculpture. Layered with textured fabric, bits of carved wood, beads, shards of polished glass, and even stones, Maxine's work had a primitive, earthy feel.

Greta let herself in and found Maxine in the kitchen dramatically stirring something in a big bowl. "You're cooking for a change?"

"Hardly. I'm making tuna salad for you. I'm having a salami-and-cheese sandwich."

Greta set her purse on the counter and proceeded to the refrigerator. She rummaged through the vegetable bin until she found some fresh carrots. "I'll cut up carrots for us. Why don't you have tuna fish?"

Maxine smeared a blob of mustard on a piece of dark rye bread. "I like salami."

Greta made a face. "But it's made out of disgusting by-products, animal parts you don't even want to think about, and it's loaded with fat."

Maxine shrugged one shoulder. "You know you just can't solve all the problems of the world with brown rice and wheat germ. And don't eat too many of your healthy sandwiches. I bought us a cheesecake for dessert."

Greta dropped a generous handful of carrot sticks on each plate. "You know, Max, maybe you'd live longer if you didn't eat so much junk."

Maxine made a face. "Listen, if I want to feel guilty, I'll call my mother. Now are we going to have an evening free of nutritional advice, or what?" Maxine picked up her plate and walked toward the living room. "You want to eat in front of the TV, don't you?"

"Sure," Greta answered. She had to remember to stop lecturing Maxine about food. It was just that Maxine was so hopelessly lost when it came to sensible eating. Greta gathered up two wineglasses and her own plate and followed Maxine.

Maxine unwrapped the foil collar from the neck of a bottle of blush wine and handed the bottle and the corkscrew to Greta. "Here, you do this. I'll get the video going."

Maxine's cat, a big orange tabby named Rembrandt,

squinted one eye at them from his perch on top of three pillows near the TV. He evidently decided that whatever food he could mooch wasn't worth the effort because he rolled over and went right back to sleep.

Maxine had rented two videos, *Broadway Danny Rose* and *Play It Again, Sam.* Both films had a lot of laughs, but even Woody Allen couldn't capture her full attention.

On and off during the evening, whenever Woody was trying to make sense of his love life, she thought about Friday's dinner with Adam. For the first time, she had seen Adam in a social setting away from the school, and she had to admit she liked what she saw. In fact, thinking about Adam was the only thing that kept her from dwelling on Belinda's death.

It was crazy, but here she was getting to know her principal on a personal level and, though her logic told her not to get involved with the boss, some other part of her kept telling her to go for it.

8

WHEN Greta arrived at school Monday morning, the TV crews were already assailing the campus, looking for gullible souls to discuss Belinda's fate. Some of the kids actually lined up for a chance to be on camera for the five o'clock news, always kids who barely knew Belinda or those who didn't know her at all. This was a side of the adolescent psyche that made Greta sick. She kept her distance from the TV vultures and their macabre groupies by circling the administration building and entering through the rear door.

Inside, the corridor was crowded for this time of morning. Avoiding a woman who looked like she might be a reporter, Greta went into the main office and initialed her time card. She noticed that with all her concern over Belinda she had forgotten to sign in or out last Friday, so she quickly filled in her usual GG in the two tiny squares.

The door to Adam's office was closed, so she couldn't stop in to thank him again for Friday's dinner as she'd planned. Perhaps she'd better let it rest. The more she thought about their evening together, the more she believed Adam had enjoyed being with her. Hadn't he called just to tell her so? But, as usual, she didn't trust her own judgment when it came to men.

After all, Carl had enjoyed her company, too. At least as

long as she'd been willing to support the two of them until he "found" himself. He bounced from job to job, from school to training program, never quite fitting in. All the while, Greta believed in him and did her best to cheer him up when yet another deal went sour. She should've wised up a lot sooner, but what the hell. Don't they say love is blind? Of course, she was damn near comatose before she figured out his game.

When he finally settled into a job he liked—bartending in a trendy singles hangout—he seemed like a new man. Now they would finally have time to work out the bugs in their marriage. Of course, she hadn't counted on old Carl's working on a few projects of his own—namely any sweet young thing who would fall for his line of bull while sipping one of his famous banana daiquiris. She had been almost too proud to quit the marriage, but in the end she recognized a dying horse when she saw one. Now she was afraid of making the same mistake twice.

She checked her mailbox, retrieving a handful of student requests for a conference with her. Belinda's death would be the topic of conversation for weeks, and they had to be prepared for some of the kids to need special crisis intervention sessions. At the very least, a support center and a crisis hot line would be set up. A team of specially trained professionals would be sent to help McCormick's counselors deal with the grief and confusion. It was going to be one hell of a week.

Stanley Deep came up from behind and lightly placed his arm around her shoulder. Some men can't just say hello. They have to make bodily contact before they even speak. Greta shrugged off his arm, making no bones about her annoyance, and turned to face him. His eyes were glassy. He looked solemn, almost afraid.

"Hi," he whispered. "Have you heard?"

"Heard what? I just got here."

"T.P. Bench was arrested last night."

Greta heard his words, but her mind wasn't ready to process

what she thought the words suggested. "What for? You don't mean . . ."

Stanley nodded. "They think he killed Belinda."

Greta felt the muscles in her throat tighten. "That's crazy. What proof do they have?"

"I don't know. I just heard the tail end of a conversation between Detective Pontrelli and the boss. Pontrelli is in there with Mason now."

"That poor kid. T.P. must be scared to death."

Stanley nodded. "I couldn't believe it either. Not a good kid like T.P."

"Shit," she said, mostly to herself. "There's got to be something we can do."

"I don't know what you can do for T.P., but there is something you can do for me," he said.

Greta eyed him suspiciously. Stanley never gave up on his offers to take her out for a "little" drink after school. He'd asked her at least twice a week ever since he started teaching at McCormick, and that was four, no five, years ago. She wasn't in the mood for Stanley's games, no matter that she would never accept any of his invitations. She doubted she would ever get that thirsty.

"What do you want, Stanley?" she finally said.

"Well, I'm not sure I can handle the kids who show up for period one. I think half the school will ditch classes today, but Algebra II is mostly seniors; they'll show up. They're going to need a chance to talk about what happened to Belinda, but I don't think I'm the person to lead this kind of rap session. I don't know what to say to them."

At least Stanley was aware of his limitations when it came to his students. She was sorry she'd been ready to accuse him of his usual lecherous conduct, but not sorry enough to tell him so.

"You want me to come over and talk to your period one class?"

"I'd consider it a tremendous favor, Greta. I'd really appreciate it." Stanley looked almost contrite. He wasn't the big bad wolf he tried to be. He was more like a child who was forced to play at a piano recital. Scared shitless.

"I'll be there at the beginning of the period," she said. "Don't worry."

"Thanks, Greta. I owe you one."

"It's part of my job. I just hope I can help."

She hurried to her office, anxious to sort through her mail and anxious to call Adam's office to talk to Pontrelli, but she saw both would have to wait. Two students, Irene Flores and Wendy Yoshimura, were already in her office waiting for her. Both had wads of tissues fisted in each hand; both looked as if they had been crying all weekend.

"Oh, Ms. Gallagher," Irene cried. "First Belinda, and now they've arrested T.P. How could they think he did it?"

Greta did not move to the chair behind her desk, but instead sat between the two girls. Irene was prettier than Belinda had been, but she was also a lot shorter. Her dimpled chin and high-pitched voice made her seem younger than many of the other senior girls, but she had a good head on her shoulders, and was a real whiz in math. At the moment Irene's tear-stained face was drawn into the worry lines of a much older person.

"I don't know, honey. I was just going to call the detective in charge of the case and ask him the same question." Greta studied the purple patches under Irene's eyes and the swollen flesh around Wendy's nose and lips. "Are you two going to be able to make it through school today? Maybe you should stay home until you feel up to schoolwork."

Wendy answered for both of them. "It's better being here with our friends, except we don't have Belinda." Wendy lowered her eyes. She was slightly pudgy but not fat. Her thick black hair hung straight to her shoulders, framing a wide face with clear, smooth skin but otherwise unremarkable features. Wendy looked miserable, as if she, too, had grown a lot older since last Friday.

Irene said, "Mrs. Jackson has to wait until Saturday or even next week for the funeral, did you know that?"

"No, I didn't," Greta answered. She weighed her words carefully. "I guess they have to examine Belinda thoroughly and run tests."

"You don't think they're cutting her up, do you? I heard the coroner does that when it's a murder."

"I'm sure that won't be necessary. They knew the cause of death, not like someone who's been poisoned." Greta bit her lip. Even as she uttered these comforting lies to Irene, she was certain Belinda's body was being sectioned by the coroner's scalpel.

Irene looked at Greta, wide-eyed, willing to believe anything that would reduce her pain. Wendy nodded solemnly, as if she also believed her friend Belinda was a special case, immune to the indignities of a postmortem.

"Tell me something," Greta said, changing the subject as quickly as possible. "Belinda was best friends with both of you, right?"

Both girls nodded, bobbing like those little toy dogs whose heads are attached with a spring.

"We all know it couldn't have been T.P., but unless it was a crazy maniac who wandered onto campus, it had to be someone who knew Belinda. At least that's what the police think. Who would want to hurt Belinda?"

Irene and Wendy looked confused. They weren't jumping to the same conclusion Greta had reached. Rudy's poking into file cards on Greta's desk and leering at the girls while he worked wasn't just her imagination. The trouble was she needed real evidence if she wanted Pontrelli off T.P.'s back and on a more likely suspect, like Rudy. She needed at least one other person who shared her suspicions.

Greta tried a different approach. "Did she fight with anyone recently? School problems, personal problems?"

This time both heads swagged back and forth in unison. Irene finally spoke up. "That policeman asked me the same question. Belinda wasn't like that. You remember, Ms. Gallagher, she was friends with everyone."

"Okay, about her friends. Did you ever see her chatting in a friendly way with any of the adults on campus besides the teachers?"

"Like who?" Irene asked.

Greta spoke slowly, watching Irene's and Wendy's eyes. "Oh, any of the workers on campus, like the security guards, the maintenance people, or even our regular custodians."

Irene shook her head. "No. She wasn't friendly with anyone like that."

Wendy chimed in, "I never saw her talk to any of the workers around school, except for that one time when her locker jammed."

"What happened when her locker jammed?" Greta asked.

Wendy shrugged. "Nothing much. She asked for help with her locker at the student store just like we're supposed to, and when they couldn't open it, they sent a custodian to fix it."

Greta's heart raced. "Do you remember which custodian fixed it?"

"Yeah, it was that young guy who's always sweeping. I think his name is Rudy."

"Did Belinda talk to Rudy?"

"Sure, we had to go to class, but Belinda waited around for him to open it. Her chemistry book was inside."

"So Rudy's pretty helpful when you girls have a problem?"

Wendy thought for a moment. "I guess. He got her locker open anyway. She was only ten minutes late for Chem."

"When was this?"

Wendy looked to Irene. "Week before last, wasn't it?"

Irene answered, "Yeah, I think so. You don't think Rudy had something to do with her murder, do you?"

"What I think doesn't matter," Greta said quickly. "The police must have solid evidence before they can make an arrest."

"So what evidence points to T.P.?"

Greta shook her head. "I don't know yet, but I do know we've got to try to think of anyone who might have had a problem with Belinda if we're going to help T.P."

Irene said, "Well, she didn't exactly have a problem with Rudy, but I don't think Belinda liked him very much. At least not the day he fixed her locker."

Greta knew this was going somewhere, but she tried not to let her own eagerness influence Irene. She tried to sound detached, as if Irene's answer didn't make the slightest difference.

"Why not?"

"Because the little creep was trying to look down Belinda's blouse the whole time she was waiting around for her chemistry book. She told me his eyes were on her boobs more than they were on the locker."

Wendy spoke up. "So what else is new? Don't we have every guy in school trying to do the same thing? Why do you think I wear turtlenecks most of the time?"

Irene touched Wendy's arm. "Ms. Gallagher isn't talking about every guy in school. We were discussing that custodian, Rudy."

"Well, then you better discuss half the teachers in this school, too. Especially Mr. Deep. He's lucky he hasn't dislocated his eyeballs," Wendy said.

Greta strained a smile. Stanley was at least true to his colors no matter who he was with. "Mr. Deep tried to look down Belinda's blouse?"

Wendy scoffed. "Not just Belinda's. He's always looking for a cheap thrill. The rule is, you wear your sweater or jacket in his class."

The warning bell signaled it was 7:50 A.M. Ten minutes until period one.

"Listen, girls, I promised Mr. Deep I'd come over to your first period. Let's not discuss what we just talked about in front of him, okay?"

"Sure," Irene answered, standing up. "We like Mr. Deep all right. He's a great math teacher. He's just sort of a dirty old man sometimes."

Greta liked the way Irene spoke her mind. This was one young lady who was not to be taken lightly. She'd probably make a good politician, or was that one of those seeming self-contradictions she taught her students to avoid?

Irene and Wendy left the office after Greta promised they could come back any time they wanted to talk. Before they could close the door behind them, Detective Pontrelli pulled it open again. He filled the doorway, standing there as if waiting for an invitation.

"I was just going to call over to the principal's office," Greta said. "I heard you arrested T.P. Bench."

"That's why I'm here," Pontrelli said, studying the wall of photographs on his right. He dug one hand deep into his pants pocket and rattled his loose change. "Mind if I sit down a minute?"

"Please do," Greta said, but not with much hospitality. "What made you decide to arrest T.P.? Don't you need all sorts of evidence to take the boy to court?"

"That's how the system works," Pontrelli said with maybe a slight note of condescension in his voice. "We gather it; the D.A. and the lawyers sort it all out."

"So what do you have on T.P.?" Greta forced herself not to raise her voice.

Pontrelli leaned back in the same chair Irene Flores had just occupied. He was dragging this out for a reason. It'd better be a good one.

"Well," he drawled, "first, the kid's got no alibi, and he's admittedly the last one to see her alive as far as we can tell. The coroner lists the time of death somewhere around five. Then, too, the kid admits they had a fight. She broke up with him just thirty, forty minutes before she died."

"But how can that be enough? Detective Pontrelli, this is a high school. We have boys and girls break up and then make up again all the time. They don't kill one another over puppy love."

"Maybe they do, maybe they don't."

Christ, she was beginning to understand how a person could be driven to murder. She gripped the edge of her desk and steadied her voice. "If they did, this campus would be littered with dead bodies. I tell you, T.P. wouldn't kill Belinda because she broke up with him."

Pontrelli scratched his chin thoughtfully. "Oh, there's one other thing. Miss Belinda Jackson, the one who was going to med school with a perfect record behind her . . ." His voice trailed off.

Greta could see herself happily strangling the words out of him. "Yes, what else?"

"Well, at the time of her death, Belinda Jackson was about three months pregnant."

9

GRETA'S mind was on fast-forward. Belinda pregnant. That was a twist she hadn't expected, but at least now she could rule out the crazed lunatic theory. Belinda's killer might have been the same man who had fathered her child—and she certainly couldn't rule out the possibility that T.P. was the father—but she still couldn't believe T.P. actually committed murder. She had learned over the years to know these kids—sometimes better than they knew themselves—and she considered herself a pretty good judge of how they would eventually turn out. Of course, she could be wrong in a case of adolescent hormones gone berserk, but some gut-level feeling still told her she could count on T.P.'s innocence.

She arrived at Stanley's classroom just as he finished taking roll. Greta noticed that Stanley had seated his students in such a way that most of the girls sat in the front of the room, while the boys occupied the chairs in the rear. None of the usual alphabetical arrangements for practical reasons, or even the less successful boy-girl, boy-girl groupings. Stanley wanted the immediate view from the teacher's desk to be as pleasantly feminine as possible. The armchair desk closest to Stanley's desk was empty, and Greta would've bet the rent it had belonged to Belinda.

The other empty chairs scattered across the front of the

room suggested that some students had taken Belinda's death pretty hard, but Greta suspected many of the absentees were just plain scared. As she talked to the more worried students, all girls, it was clear that, horrified as they were by what had happened to Belinda, there was also a sense of relief that it hadn't happened to any of them.

Stanley closed his roll book and made a quick effort to tidy the surface of his desk, neatly lining up his pens and pencils, and organizing a stack of student papers. Greta didn't bother to tell him she wouldn't be using his desk. The desk would distance her from the students. She pulled up a straight-backed chair and placed it close to the front row, almost knee-to-knee with Irene.

Stanley got up from his desk. "Where do you want me to sit?"

"Anywhere you like," she answered.

Stanley took the stack of student papers and his roll book to an empty seat in the very last row. Greta encouraged the kids sitting in the back to move forward and fill the empty seats, forming a more intimate grouping.

For the full hour, Greta encouraged the students to talk about their feelings even though this approach opened a floodgate of tears. Most of the boys tried to hide their reddened eyes, but some were willing to let the tears flow. By the end of the period, Irene and Wendy and a few other girls who had known Belinda best hugged and consoled each other. It had been a good session. Greta finally noticed that, at some point during the hour, Stanley had slipped out of the room, probably in search of a second cup of coffee.

When the bell rang, Stanley's students went on to their next classes, and Greta walked over to Maxine's classroom. Period two was Maxine's conference period, so there was a pretty good chance she might be in her room alone. Thank God she was.

Just as she did when entering Maxine's condo, Greta sensed

a collision course with visual stimuli during every visit to Maxine's classroom. Posters screaming bright primary colors outlined with slashes of black and white plastered the walls. More bold paintings were somehow stapled to the acoustical tiles on the ceiling. Whimsical mobiles fashioned out of bits of cardboard, smashed aluminum cans, and everyday items such as plastic combs dangled from every light fixture, twirling in the air currents from the ventilator. One small bulletin board displayed a more subtle collection of watercolors done in pastel shades, mostly landscapes.

"I like these," Greta said, pointing to the watercolors.

Maxine looked up from the paper cutter she wielded like an executioner. Her hair, storming in all directions, resembled the pile of shredded yellow tissue on the table next to her. "Yeah, me, too. Painting and Drawing did those last week. I've got a few really talented kids in that class."

Greta glanced at some of the signatures on the paintings. One exceptionally lovely watercolor had been painted by a boy in her fourth-period lit class. Barely passing Greta's class, the boy hated to read and went to great lengths to avoid writing more than a paragraph on his essay assignments. The few words he tried to pass off as a composition were forced—and barely legible, to boot. She was delighted that a student who did so poorly in English class positively shone in art, but what did that do to her theory that she knew her students better than they knew themselves? No, this one incident wasn't proof enough to shake her confidence in T.P.

Greta turned away from the watercolors and walked back to Maxine. "I talked to Pontrelli this morning. He told me Belinda was pregnant."

Maxine forced the blade of the paper cutter through many folded layers of bright red tissue paper and brought the handle to rest with a thud. "No shit?"

Greta nodded. "And I talked to two of Belinda's friends. They said Belinda was alone with Rudy Smith one day last week. He fixed her locker."

"So? Fixing a locker doesn't make him public enemy number one."

"I know, but he bothers me. Those shifty, beady eyes of his give me the creeps."

Maxine shot Greta a worried look. "Beady eyes didn't make Belinda pregnant. I think you're wasting your time trying to play detective."

"Don't tell me you think T.P. is guilty, too?"

"Hell, I don't know, but doesn't her pregnancy make you wonder? Maybe T.P. invented that story about her breaking up with him. Maybe she wanted to have an abortion and he didn't want her to."

Greta sat on the edge of one of the tables. "Most likely the other way around."

"Sure, and if Belinda wanted to have the kid, and the father had a problem with that . . ."

Greta spoke slowly. "Yes, but what if she got mixed up with someone other than T.P.? Someone older who could lose his job for fooling around with one of the students?"

Maxine sighed. "Okay, I see where you're going with this. But don't you see that it could apply to every male employed on this campus? From the lowly Rudy Smith all the way up to your friend Adam."

Greta ignored the dig about Adam. "Rudy isn't that much older than Belinda was, and Rudy wouldn't have as much to lose if he got involved with a student. I think the professional men on our staff, including Adam, would have more sense."

"Listen, if they've got a zipper in their pants and they can still get it up, that's all the sense they've got."

Greta jumped from her perch on the table and started

pacing. "How long is it going to take before you stop bashing men?"

"Hey, I like men. Some of them. Don't I have a date with the union rep from Kennedy High next Saturday?"

"Only because I talked you into it."

"Hey, I try. Just because I was married to the world's biggest jerk for three years doesn't mean I can't forgive and forget."

Greta stopped walking and faced Maxine. "Well, Carl was no prize either, but they're not all bad."

"The one who did Belinda was."

A sudden weakness fluttered down Greta's legs, lodging in her knees. One of these days she would have to start eating a bigger breakfast.

Greta said, "I'd better get back to the office. Vera is probably searching for me."

Maxine placed her hands on Greta's shoulders. "Smart I'm not, at least not at first. You're falling for Adam, aren't you? And that crack I made about Adam being no better than Rudy pissed you off."

Greta's head drooped forward. "It's idiotic to think there could ever be anything between Adam and me on the basis of one dinner, isn't it?"

"Sure, but that doesn't have anything to do with it. If you feel your gut wrenching over Adam, there's nothing you can do about it. Love is a lot like diarrhea."

Greta hugged Maxine. "Thanks for listening, but I do have to get back to the office. I'll talk to you later." She headed for the door but then turned to face Maxine. "Don't say anything to anyone, all right?"

"Do I look like a crazy person? I would tell people my best friend has the hots for a principal?"

Greta smiled to herself as she hurried back to her office. A few birds chattered in a tree and a squirrel scolded from behind the base of a bottlebrush shrub. The ground cover planted between the shrubs had been trampled by kids taking a shortcut through the bushes on their way to class. Only the toughest forms of life survived on a high school campus.

The walkways were quiet, a good sign the teachers were managing to keep the lid on. No one would get in a whole lot of teaching today, but then subject matter wasn't important at this point. Dealing with Belinda's death was.

Greta glanced at her watch. She had so much to do, she really shouldn't waste another second. The crisis counselors were due to arrive at ten. They would give Greta and the other counselors a hand with the one-to-one counseling as the need arose, and they would also set up a crisis hot line as soon as the phone company had a few new lines in place.

She rounded the corner at the end of the history building and stopped dead. At the other end of the building, Irene Flores stood talking to Rudy Smith. Their heads were too close together for this to be a quick hello. Greta walked closer, thinking, trying to come up with something to say that wouldn't make Rudy question her intrusion.

"Irene," Greta called, "I hope you weren't looking for me. I've been out of my office since the beginning of period two." She looked at Rudy. "Hello," she said casually.

Irene turned toward Greta and smiled. Rudy didn't say hello, nor did he say anything else to Irene. He simply lowered his dark, angry eyes and scurried around the corner, out of sight. Like a rat slinking off in the night, Greta thought. Her heart pounded at the thought of what this encounter between Rudy and Irene might mean. Whatever they had discussed, they sure as hell weren't talking about who was or wasn't going to the Friday night dance.

"What are you doing out of class?" Greta asked Irene.

Irene studied the toes of her shoes. "I've been walking

around in circles since I left Mr. Deep's room. I just couldn't deal with P.E. today."

"So you cut class?"

"I'm sorry, Ms. Gallagher. I should have come to you, but I guess I just wanted to be alone so I could think."

"Well, do you feel any better?" Greta realized her tone was a bit sharp. She wanted to be sympathetic, but she couldn't very well openly condone truancy.

Irene's eyes brimmed with tears. "I guess so. I'm not sure how I feel. When you talked to my algebra class, and we cried and hugged one another, that felt good, but I can't get the thought of what Belinda must look like out of my mind. Oh, Ms. Gallagher, I don't even want to go to her funeral."

Greta put her arm around Irene and steered her toward the administration building. "You don't have to go to the funeral if you don't want to. You can remember Belinda as she was when she was alive."

Irene nodded, following along in silence wherever Greta led her.

Rudy had disappeared completely, but Greta was not through with him yet. She had to know why Rudy had cornered Irene.

"Did the custodian ask to see your hall pass?" she asked. "I guess he's been told to be on the lookout for wandering students."

Irene hesitated, then said, "No, we just talked. He was real friendly . . . like he cared about what happened to Belinda. I was surprised."

"Surprised that he was friendly?"

"No, that he knew Belinda and I had been close. He said he was real sorry to hear about what had happened to my friend."

"Was that all he said?"

Irene hesitated again, this time twisting a lock of her hair tightly around her finger. "Yeah. No, he said if I needed anything, like if my locker jammed or something, he'd be happy to help me out."

She'd just bet he would. "Why don't you lie down in the health office for a little while? I'll tell the nurse to give you a pass when you feel like going back to class."

"Thanks, Ms. Gallagher."

Greta spoke with the nurse and left Irene in her hands. The main office was right across the hall from the nurse's, so she headed inside and went directly to the principal's door.

Adam looked up when she burst into the room.

"Adam, I've got to talk to you, privately."

He got up from his desk, motioned for her to sit, and closed the door to his office almost in one continuous movement. "I don't suppose this can wait until dinner tonight?"

"What?"

"Will you have dinner with me tonight?"

The words caught in her throat. "Oh, sure, that would be great, thank you, but I really wanted to talk to you now."

Adam sat down again and smiled. "Talk away. I guess you heard Belinda Jackson was pregnant."

"Yes, but I think the police have arrested the wrong person. I don't think T.P. was the father of her child any more than I can believe he killed her. Something about this whole thing just isn't right."

The smile on Adam's face faded. "So who do you suppose was the father?"

"Well," Greta said, "I have no proof, but I do have a theory."

"Tell me."

Adam's office was too warm. She wished she had removed her blazer, but it would be awkward to do so now. Adam wore a suit jacket and he didn't seem uncomfortable. She concentrated on the little speech she had been rehearsing in her mind since she left Irene.

"Well," Greta began, "I think Belinda grew tired of T.P. as so many girls do when they suddenly realize they've matured a lot faster than their boyfriends. When that happens, they seek out someone who is older."

Adam thought for a moment. "Some college kid, perhaps?"

Greta hesitated, then said, "Oh, I don't know. Why not someone she met right here on campus? An older man who flattered her by showing interest in a seventeen-year-old. It happens all the time."

"You don't mean one of her teachers?"

Greta met Adam's gaze. "It's happened before, hasn't it?"

"Well sure," Adam answered, steepling his fingers under his chin, "but there's nothing to substantiate such a claim in this case. Nothing has come up about Belinda fooling around with one of her teachers, has it?"

Greta had known Adam wouldn't buy the teacher theory. She didn't buy it herself, but it gave her an opportunity to lead into her suspicions about Rudy. Adam was the only one, besides Detective Pontrelli, of course, who carried any weight in the investigation.

"Okay," she said, "so maybe not a teacher. How about someone else? Maybe one of the custodians."

Adam gave her a puzzled look, like he was thinking she had finally sharpened one too many pencils. "What would a young girl like Belinda see in a custodian? They're all quite a bit older than her crowd."

Greta jumped right into the opening Adam had given her. "Rudy Smith can't be more than five years older. He may have handed her a line of sweet talk. You never know."

"Rudy Smith? Well, he's one I wouldn't have thought of myself."

Greta said, "I think we owe it to Belinda to check out all the possibilities, don't you?"

"That's what the police are doing, aren't they?"

Greta bit the insides of her cheeks and swallowed hard. Adam would surely withdraw his dinner invitation any moment. She might end up kicking herself for this one. Finally she just spat it out. "Why don't you suggest to Pontrelli that the police department run a check on Rudy?"

Adam hesitated. Did he feel she'd backed him into a corner? He got up and walked over to her. "Do you have some basis for your suspicions you haven't told me about?"

"Mostly gut feelings."

"I think the police need more than that to go on."

"Well, they've got no other clues, so everything revolves around Belinda's pregnancy. What can it hurt to at least find out if Rudy's ever been in trouble?"

Adam chewed on his lower lip for a second. "I guess it can't hurt anyone if the police are thorough."

"Then you'll talk to Pontrelli?"

"Why not? Who knows, you may be onto something."

"Thanks," Greta said.

Adam smiled. "Maybe you'll explain your theories to me tonight. Is seven okay?"

"Yes."

"I'll pick you up at your house if that's all right."

"Fine. Seven, at my house."

Greta walked down the corridor to the counseling office, her heels echoing against the hard vinyl tile. She should be happy, shouldn't she? Adam was definitely interested in her. They were having dinner again tonight, and this time it was actually a date. Adam was even going to urge Pontrelli to look into Rudy Smith's background. Everything was going the way she wanted. So then why did she feel as if all her bodily functions had collapsed into slow motion, leaving her with a heaviness that sank all the way down to her toes?

10

GRETA was ready when Adam arrived at seven. She got into his car, her heart pulsing with anticipation. This was not her boss, the principal, but Adam the man. She remembered his gentle, smooth-talking manner from dinner last Friday, so different from the principal she generally tried to avoid at school. What if her memory had been distorted by the stress of first finding Belinda and then dealing with Pontrelli? Once they covered the conventional small talk and then, of course, the murder, what could they possibly have in common? A real date with Adam could be dreadful, like her very first date way back in junior high school when she spent the entire evening so tongue-tied she felt pimples erupting one by one across her nose.

Adam smiled as she settled into the bucket seat and hooked her seat belt. "Greta, you look great. You should always wear blue."

Greta's fears dissolved and she made a mental note to buy only blue clothes from now on. She relaxed, not even remembering what she had been worried about in the first place.

He drove over the canyon to a trendy French bistro in Beverly Hills. Greta had read about this restaurant in the *L.A. Times*, but it was not the kind of place you frequent on a teacher's salary. The interior dripped with Art Deco chic. High windows flanked abstract paintings done in bright pinks, shades of purple, and black. Mauve tablecloths reached almost to the floor, which was carpeted in black with pink and mauve designs. A black ceramic vase on each table held one perfect pink rose. They sat in a little alcove surrounded by potted palms and the kind of waiters who unfold the napkin and drape it over your lap for you.

Even if she ordered the least expensive item, dinner was going to cost Adam plenty. She shifted her weight in her chair as she skimmed the pricy menu, but Adam seemed unconcerned, as if he ate three meals a day here, seven days a week.

"Not as homey as Maria's, but the food is excellent. They have several seafood dishes I really like," Adam said. "You do eat fish, don't you?"

"Yes," Greta answered, pleased that Adam remembered her food preferences.

"Good, then let me order a wonderful white wine they have here. It's one of those special labels you can't find in the stores."

"That's fine with me."

What did Greta know about labels you can't find in the stores? She and Maxine bought wine at Hughes Market, and it always had the kind of label everybody in town recognized. Cheap stuff.

Adam ordered the wine and an appetizer, stuffed mushroom caps.

"I love the way they do mushrooms here," he said. "They're one of my favorites. Reminds me of something I had once in Marseilles." He paused. "I don't mean to sound like a well-traveled name-dropper."

"Drop away," she said. "I like to talk about the places I've visited."

"Did you want me to order for you?"

Greta closed her menu. "No, thanks. I know exactly what I'm going to have. I didn't suffer through high school French for nothing."

Adam laughed. He was awfully easy to talk to. And he didn't seem to be playing cat-and-mouse games like some of the men she had dated since her divorce. At first, she'd withdrawn into a protective shell and devoted herself entirely to her work. Mostly at Maxine's urging, she'd gradually entered the singles' scene. She'd met a lot of men in their thirties, many recently divorced themselves, and as soon as they met the games began. Honesty and openness were something they reserved for their analysis sessions, and no one would commit to a relationship that might last longer than a one-night stand.

But Adam was different. She guessed he was at least forty-five, though his age didn't matter. She was ready for someone more mature. Suddenly she remembered her theory about Belinda outgrowing her seventeen-year-old high school sweetheart, wanting to be swept off her feet by someone who knew what the world was all about. Maybe it would have happened anyway, but there was no question Belinda's misfortune had been the catalyst that had brought Adam and her together.

"You ever been to Paris?" Adam asked.

"Yes, I love France."

"I've always wanted to live abroad for a year or two, just to soak up the ambience in a city like Paris."

"Who wouldn't? But Paris has its share of problems, too, you know. Traffic jams, crime, smog. It's not all wine and escargot."

"Yes, I know. I just get carried away with my daydreams sometimes. Maybe I'm ready for a major change in my life," Adam said.

Greta blotted her lips with her napkin and pretended her mouth was too full to respond. Why was he confiding that he wanted a change in his life? Why was she reading six volumes into every sentence he spoke?

"I was wondering if you'd like to go to a play over the weekend."

"Sure, I'd love to. You have anything in particular in mind?"

"What do you prefer, dramas or musicals?"

"Actually, I prefer a good comedy, but I also enjoy drama—especially a good mystery."

"You trust me to come up with something on my own, or do you want to check out the calendar section of the *Times* before I buy tickets?"

"I trust you."

Adam grinned. Obviously, she had said the right thing.

When the waiter suggested coffee, Adam leaned closer to Greta. "Why don't we have coffee at my place? I make a mean espresso."

A tingling sensation quivered up her spine. Hordes of illogical fantasies invaded the logical part of her mind. The fear of AIDS had pretty much crushed her sexual appetite for men she didn't know well, but this was not the case with Adam. She was definitely attracted to him. How could she be so eager for a sexual encounter on just their second date? Of course, if she were entirely honest with herself, she would have to admit she had been ready on their *first* evening together. Was this chemistry, or had she simply gone without sex for too long? God, she was reacting like a kid, gooseflesh and all.

A short time later, Adam pulled into the circular drive in front of his Laurel Canyon home. Now Greta understood why Adam was not concerned about the price of dinner. The place was a mansion, and the entire San Fernando Valley lay like a carpet of sparkling lights beneath the hillside home. The moon hung huge and low over the valley as if Adam had ordered it up for the occasion just to impress her.

"Wow, the view from here is gorgeous," Greta said.

Adam helped her out of the car. A breeze stirred the scent of something exotic in their direction. "Mmm, something smells wonderful," Greta said. "What is it?"

"Night-blooming jasmine. Come inside." He slipped his arm neatly around her waist.

The move was natural enough, but Greta tensed, her back stiffening. She hoped Adam hadn't felt it. All logic told her that dating her principal did not automatically make her a Mata Hari. Damn that Maxine. It was Maxine's fault she felt like a traitor.

Greta followed Adam inside. He went straight to a panel of wall switches and, with a few quick flicks, illuminated the enormous living room in front of her. A tiny beam of light shot out of the ceiling and rested on an expensive-looking oil painting over the fireplace. Indirect lighting flashed on behind the books on the top shelf of a wide built-in bookcase, and lights twinkled from gadgets rigged inside every potted plant in the room. The effect was dramatic, but the room was still barely lit.

Next he approached a unit that she suspected housed a sound system to rival that of the Hollywood Bowl. A few properly punched buttons flipped a CD into place and a low melody drifted from strategically hidden speakers. If Adam's equipment was any indication, he was no stranger to the art of seduction.

"I'll be right back with the espresso," Adam said. "Make yourself at home."

"You didn't tell me you lived in a palace."

"It is kind of too much for one person. I like it better when I have company."

Greta smiled, wondering how anyone ever felt at home in the Taj Mahal. She walked gingerly across the living room, fearful of tripping when her heels disappeared into the deep pile of the carpeting. She headed for a sectional sofa that sprawled in front of the floor-to-ceiling windows on one wall.

She couldn't help thinking that the area covered by this one sofa was larger than her entire living room.

She nestled into the soft, velvety cushions and stared straight ahead. It was hard to take her eyes from the view, but she also found this was not a room one could take in just at a glance. A fireplace flickered over to her right in a little conversation pit. Had Adam ignited the flame with one of his buttons, or had it been burning all along? The majestic glass-topped coffee table in front of her must have cost a small fortune. It held a single item, a small piece of sculpture carved out of white marble. Greta ran her fingertips over the smooth milky surface, then immediately wondered if it was too valuable for such casual handling. She had no idea who had created the exquisite figure of a woman, but she was certain it was an original.

What she had seen of the house so far confirmed the rumors she had heard at school about Adam's wife having been the heiress to a considerable fortune her father had made in an import-export business. Whatever the source of Adam's prosperity, it had to be something other than a principal's salary.

He returned carrying a small tray with the espresso and two tiny cups. Greta noticed that Adam had removed his jacket and necktie. When he sat next to her and filled the cups, a faint odor of chocolate mingled with the stronger coffee scent. She sipped slowly, feeling the warm steam against her face.

"This is wonderful," she said. "Did they teach you this in principal's school?"

Adam laughed. He put his feet up on the glass tabletop, crossing his legs at the ankles. "I like your sense of humor. Shows you aren't all business. I like that in a woman. People are too damned uptight these days."

If he only knew how uptight she really felt. She kept her eyes on the heels of Adam's shoes, hoping he was not marring the delicate glass. She decided to relax even if it killed her. She slipped out of her shoes and tucked her legs beneath her.

"You shouldn't hide such shapely ankles," Adam said. "I've enjoyed watching you walk this evening. But then I've watched you walk on campus many times. Did you ever catch me observing you?"

"No," Greta answered, staring into her cup for fear of doing something stupid like swooning. "I didn't notice you watching me."

With that, Adam removed his feet from the table and inched closer. His warm breath tickled her cheek.

Adam leaned over and kissed her lightly, but firmly, on the mouth. At once she was floating somewhere in a puff of clouds. She wanted the moment to go on, but he withdrew and moved back, just enough to give her air. God, she needed CPR. She was certain her heart had stopped beating.

Adam whispered, "I knew that would be nice; instead it was magnificent."

The logical corner of Greta's brain shut down completely. It had been so many years since a mere kiss had affected her like that. This made no sense. She was falling in love faster than she could think. The witty remark that was supposed to follow Adam's compliment died in her throat. She simply looked at him and smiled like an obedient child.

"I'm a little rusty; you'll have to be patient with me," he said.

"That should be easy. I'm very comfortable with you." Shit, she hadn't meant to say that. Why was she such a bubblehead all of a sudden? She studied his clean-shaven, almost rugged profile. Right now he was her gladiator, and she was ready to jump into his chariot if he would only ask.

"You're very lovely, and I find myself genuinely attracted to you. I thought when I lost Helen I was done with romance. Now I know better." He kissed her again.

Greta's spine melted into the sofa waiting for his lovemaking to proceed, but again he backed off. "You must have loved Helen very much," she finally whispered.

"Yes, she was a wonderful woman, very creative. She painted a little, wrote poetry, cooked gourmet meals for two or twenty. There was very little she couldn't do."

"I'm so sorry you lost her. It was a fall that killed her, wasn't it?"

"Yes," he answered. Even in the dim light, Greta could see him gaze off into the distance. "A careless slip on the top step of a flight of stairs. We had a vacation home up at Lake Arrowhead. That's where it happened."

"How dreadful."

"I sold the place right after. Took a tremendous loss on the property, but I couldn't bear to look at that staircase after her accident."

"I'm so sorry."

Adam nodded, but he did not meet Greta's eyes. "It's all right, really. We had a good life together, but I have to go on living. Helen would have been pleased I connected with someone like you."

Greta's cheeks grew warm. Thank God Adam couldn't see her embarrassment in the near darkness. Adam was the first widower she had ever dated, and this was a new experience. None of the divorced men she had known had ever spoken kindly about an ex-wife.

"Helen decorated the house beautifully," Greta said with a sweep of her arm. "Your living room is elegant, reminds me of a movie set, especially with your spectacular view."

"Yes, I enjoy the view. It's even better upstairs, from my bedroom. You can see over all those trees practically down to Ventura Boulevard."

"Really? I'll bet it's pretty at night." She had wondered how he would invite her to his bed, but it didn't matter. After the first kiss, she was his, just like the heroine in one of those corny romance novels from the fifties.

Adam slid forward on the cushions and lightly squeezed her knee. "I'll show you my own private view when we have more time, but now I guess I'd better get you home. I had no idea it was so late. We have a school to run tomorrow."

Greta tried to check her watch, but it was too dark. She'd been too eager. She had to give Adam time to get used to the idea of a new woman in his life. Hadn't he asked her to be patient?

She found her shoes and slid her feet into them. When she stood, Adam put his arms around her and gave her a lingering kiss. "This could become habit-forming."

"I certainly hope so," she said.

They drove down the gradual hill to the main street in Studio City in a dreamy sort of silence. Greta was now relaxed, confident her relationship with Adam was going somewhere. A calm spot somewhere in her head felt warm and good. No denying she was extremely happy.

Before they reached her house, Adam cleared his throat and said, "I don't want to bring up an unpleasant subject, but I forgot to tell you I asked Detective Pontrelli to investigate Rudy Smith."

"What did Pontrelli say?"

"He said you had indicated something to him last Friday about Rudy fingering Belinda's files in your office. You didn't tell me that."

"I thought I did," she lied. "He touched her program card, left a grease smudge on it. Not much of a clue, but it bothered me at the time."

"Well, Pontrelli said he was checking into a lot of people, including Rudy, but, nevertheless, he thought he had a pretty good case against T.P."

"He just wants to get this investigation over with as soon as possible," Greta said. "When the case is closed, he's off the hook."

"I don't know about Pontrelli's motives, but he could be right about T.P."

"Nope. I know that boy. He's gentle, almost shy. He's not a killer."

"Still, I wish you'd back off. Let the cops do what they have to do to get this thing solved."

"I think we have a sicko who's after young girls, and Rudy Smith could be the one."

"Making an unsupported statement like that could get you into all kinds of hot water, you know."

Greta choked back a few expletives. "Why do you want me to back off? To get the ten o'clock news teams off campus?"

Adam's expression seemed to harden, or maybe it was just the way the shadows cast by the streetlights fell across his face. He gripped the steering wheel a little harder and spoke a little louder. "It has nothing to do with the news or the campus or, for that matter, even with me. I just don't want you to get hurt."

"Why would I get hurt? I'm not a seventeen-year-old cheerleader who's romping with some sex deviate."

"Greta, you're not hearing me. Let's just say, for the sake of argument, that you're right. Suppose Belinda did get involved with an older man."

"Like Rudy?"

"Like Rudy or even someone else. The killer, if it isn't T.P., would be watching what happens, maybe even noticing you've got your suspicions. Certainly he would get wind of any accusations of this sort, especially if you make the mistake of repeating to others what you've told me."

Greta said, "So, you're afraid I'm going to make him nervous."

"Yes. Nervous to the point he may have to silence you, one way or the other."

11

TUESDAY morning was warm, and strong Santa Ana winds rolled in from the desert, howling across the campus. Greta sidestepped an empty aluminum soda can clattering along in the breeze. Trash and leaves blew against the exterior doors of the administration building and, with every opening, swept inside, forming dusty little whorls on the corridor floor.

The students automatically raised their voices on days like this, shouting and shoving one another in rhythm to the bellowing winds.

"They're gonna be high as kites today," Vera announced.

Greta smiled at Vera. Nothing was going to ruin her mood today, not even Vera or the roaring Santa Anas. "But at least the winds have blown away the smog. Have you ever seen the sky so blue?"

Vera peered at her, her features knit together in a disapproving frown. According to Vera, people were supposed to gripe about the weather first thing in the morning. Vera didn't know any other way to start the day. It was either too hot or too cold, too windy, or God forbid, if it was raining, too wet. Greta's sanity would be immediately suspect if she didn't agree with Vera's complaints about the elements, but today Greta didn't care what Vera thought.

"Any news from the police?" Greta asked.

Vera puffed out her ample chest. "T.P. gets charged with Belinda's murder today." There was nothing Vera liked better than being the bearer of rotten news.

Poor T.P. Greta tried not to think about the quiet boy whose life might never again be the same, and got right to work helping Vera readmit yesterday's absentee students.

"And you got a call from a parent on the school-based management team. Note's on your desk. Wanted to know how all this was going to affect your planning for more parent involvement."

"I wish I knew," Greta said.

They processed a few pupils, then Vera moved from her usual spot in the center of the counter closer to the end where Greta stood.

Vera said, "I couldn't help hearing yesterday. Your voice carried right out into the center of the office."

"What?"

"Just what you asked those two girls about Belinda and Rudy. You don't really think Rudy did it, do you?"

Greta threw Vera a desperate glance. "You're not repeating this to anyone, are you?" Not for a minute did she buy the part about her voice carrying. Vera must have been perched right outside Greta's door.

"No, of course not. I wouldn't tell a soul."

She'd bet Vera could keep something like that to herself. Just like King Kong could keep his hands off a big banana. Adam had been right—she needed to be more careful.

During the first three class periods, Greta planned to return telephone calls to parents who had left messages. The calls, with a few exceptions, focused on Belinda. Parents demanded to know what was being done.

Had school security been beefed up? Definitely. Extra security guards now patrolled the campus from three to six each afternoon in addition to the two new guards added to the daytime force.

Would T.P. be permitted back into school if he was released on bail? Greta didn't have the answer to that one, but she tried to assure parents that school was going on as usual in spite of the tragedy.

Second period Maxine bolted into Greta's office and slammed the door shut so hard the window rattled.

"Why didn't you call me last night?" Maxine said. She fell into one of the wooden chairs and waited.

Greta looked up from the note she had been reading. "What are you trying to do? It takes them six weeks to replace a broken window around here."

"I waited up last night, to hear about your date."

"I got in pretty late. I was afraid you'd be asleep."

Maxine pulled a hefty wad of gum from her mouth and snatched up a sheet of paper from Greta's waste can. She wrapped the gum in the paper, just the way they teach students to do, and tossed it in the trash. "So what kind of torture is this? Tell me already."

"We went to Pierre's in Beverly Hills and had a wonderful dinner."

"At least he's not cheap," Maxine said. "So then what?"

"We went back to his place for espresso. You should see the view from his living room, Max, and his house is gorgeous. Must be worth over a million, maybe two million."

Maxine swept her hair back out of her face. "I don't have time for his financial report. Skip to the good stuff."

"Well, he kissed me."

"Did he force himself on you?" Maxine demanded. "I'll bet he's a pushy son of a bitch."

Greta smiled. "He's a perfect gentleman. I had a lovely evening."

Maxine scratched her head. "I thought he'd be an animal. All over you."

"That would have been nice, but all that happened was a few lingering kisses."

"I give my cat lingering kisses."

Greta said, "Give us time. Remember, he's still getting over the death of his wife."

"Christ, don't tell me you spent the evening talking about a dead woman."

"No, but—" The phone rang. "I'll talk to you later, Max. Okay?" Greta picked up the phone. "Counseling Office, Ms. Gallagher."

Maxine left more quietly than she had entered, and Greta got back to her call. Another parent wanted to know if it was safe to send her daughter to school.

A few minutes before fourth period, Greta gathered her purse and book bag and headed for her classroom. She noticed her reflection in the glass door of the administration building as she pushed it open. Her tailored suit seemed out-of-date, too dowdy. Perhaps Adam would get turned on by something softer, more feminine. She had to remember to ask Maxine to go shopping with her over the weekend. Max had a real flair for putting outfits together, even though her own were just this side of outrageous most of the time.

Greta approached the English building. The yellow police line tapes had been removed from around the teachers' workroom, but in Greta's mind they would always be there, just as she would always visualize the workroom door slightly ajar. The fine hairs on the back of her neck bristled at the memory of Belinda lying there. She hurried past the workroom to the classroom she shared with Cecelia Hartman.

The passing bell rang and a noisy throng of students thundered out of the room. Cecelia was scribbling something on the chalkboard when Greta walked inside. Greta suddenly understood why she had grown unhappy with the tailored look of her clothes. She looked just like Cecelia. Except for Cecelia's fussy white blouse with a flounce of lace at the neck (Greta wore a thin cotton sweater) they were dressed the same. Their suits were different colors and fabrics, but the businesslike cut was identical. Her need to go shopping escalated to a level of desperation.

Cecelia looked up. "There you are. I was wondering if you could ask your students not to move the chairs around so much. Yesterday the first two rows were completely out of line."

Just then a gusting wind slammed the door shut with a loud thud, completely unnerving Cecelia.

"I hate days like this," Cecelia said. She ran to prop open the door once again.

Greta looked for a spot to unload her book bag, but decided to wait. Cecelia was neurotic, bitching about something as trivial as the alignment of the chairs. Maxine would say that Cecelia needed to get laid, and at the moment, Greta was almost willing to agree with that assessment.

"I'll tell the kids to put the chairs back the way you want them," Greta said. "Yesterday, I was so preoccupied with Belinda and T.P., I guess I didn't even notice."

"Did you see the mess the police made in our workroom?" Cecelia pressed her thin lips together into a tight seal.

Greta shook her head. "It'll be a long time before I go into that room again, for any reason."

Greta's fourth-period students began to arrive, tiptoeing around Cecelia to take their seats.

"Well," Cecelia went on, "I cleaned up the mess and put everything back in order, but I can't see why they had to disturb our supplies. They even moved the overhead and the movie projector away from the wall."

"Maybe they were trying to solve a murder," Greta said.

"I for one will be very happy when this campus returns to

normal." Cecelia picked up a neat stack of papers on the edge of the desk and hurried out of the room.

Greta knew, with only two classes per day, she had no choice but to share a classroom with another teacher. She had secretly hoped some of Cecelia's tidiness would rub off on her, but so far that hadn't happened. She constantly had to police her students to make sure they didn't mess up Cecelia's orderly system.

The tardy bell signaled the beginning of fourth period. A few minutes later, three students dashed into the room and lunged into their seats, laughing, their faces flushed with excitement. She'd let them slide. It was easier than trying to unearth the reasons for this misdemeanor. Besides, her feelings toward Adam had mellowed the disciplinarian in her. Perhaps she should feel guilty for all the happiness in her heart in light of what had happened to Belinda, but Adam's recent attention had left her feeling frivolous, like she was ready to break out in song. Right now she just wanted to glide around the room like Ginger Rogers with Fred Astaire, except dancing down the aisles would bump the rows of chairs out of alignment, and *The Scarlet Letter* would not get discussed.

The wind continued to howl. Dust-filled air thrummed through the ventilator, droning as it caught against the fan. Greta's students were much noisier than usual; pencils kept dropping, books fell to the floor. When the bell announced it was time for fourth period to go to lunch, Greta was ready for a break.

In the teachers' cafeteria, the noise level was extreme. Did everyone else sense the tension in the air, or was she just premenstrual? Greta bought a cup of vegetable soup and a grilled cheese sandwich and sat down at one of the long Formica tables. Adam usually walked around the grounds at lunch, chatting with students while he kept an eye open for problems. Perhaps she would join him later and stroll with him as he made his rounds. She hoped she wasn't exaggerating his interest in her. Of course not. *He* had kissed *her*, hadn't he?

"Hey, you look deep in thought."

Greta looked up. Stanley had taken the chair directly across from her. She wasn't in the mood for Stanley, but then she was seldom in the mood for Stanley. "Hi," she said flatly.

"Any news about T.P.?" he asked.

"Vera said they were going to formally charge him today, but I haven't heard any more."

Stanley slathered some butter on a roll. "I guess that means the police are convinced T.P. did it."

"They're convinced. I'm not," Greta said.

Stanley removed a few slices of cooked ham from a plastic bag and placed it on the roll. Greta never could understand why he didn't put his sandwiches together at home. He bit into his sandwich and chewed.

"This morning's paper said Belinda was pregnant." Stanley sounded a lot like a judge reading a death sentence.

"That doesn't necessarily mean T.P. fathered the child—or that he killed her."

Stanley swished his tongue over his teeth, dislodging food particles from his gums. "Come on, Greta."

"I mean it. T.P. admitted their love life was on the rocks. She could have been seeing someone else."

"All the more reason for T.P. to lose his cool, I'd say."

Greta shook her head. "Not T.P. Look, Stanley, this isn't the work of an outraged kid who went nuts in a moment of anger. The body was hidden. How would T.P. get the door to the workroom open?"

"He stole a key."

"That's ridiculous. The killer already had a key, and it wasn't T.P.—or any of our students, for that matter."

"You limit your killer to those who have keys, you're talking about a member of the faculty."

"Or the staff," Greta said, remembering not to air her suspicions where others might overhear.

"Nah, keys can be lifted too easily around here, and you give these kids too much credit. At that age they're just a kettle of stewing hormones. You never know what they're capable of doing."

Greta wasn't in the mood for an argument, but in Stanley's case she'd make an exception. She started to disagree, but just then a tremendous uproar outside the teachers' cafeteria stopped her in mid-sentence. Loud screaming and shouting pulled every teacher in the room to his or her feet. At least thirty adults rushed to the door.

Greta squeezed through the doorway and saw Adam grab Juan Ballestero by the arm. Juan looked dazed. He staggered like a big, gangly rag doll, all loose, as if he were ready to collapse. Greta noticed red smears on the front of Juan's shirt. Blood. He must have gotten into a fight.

Wendy Yoshimura stood off to Juan's left screaming uncontrollably. Her eyes were swollen from crying; she had a wild, delirious look on her face. The other students drew into tight clusters, pressing closer and closer to the center of activity. Several teachers herded the kids away from Juan and Wendy. No one gave any orders to that effect, but teachers are trained to discourage large crowds whenever trouble erupts.

Greta pushed through the knots of students and finally reached Adam and Juan. "What happened?" she shouted over the noise.

Juan looked at her as if she were a total stranger. She had a sinking feeling Juan was in shock.

Another teacher escorted Wendy closer. Wendy stopped screaming when her eyes focused on Greta, and she began to cry hysterically.

"What the hell's going on?" Adam demanded.

Greta put both her arms around Wendy. "Calm down, honey. It's all right. Just tell us what happened."

Wendy's whole body heaved with sobs. Her face looked twisted, more frightened than hurt. Greta shushed her in a crooning sort of whisper. After a few moments, Wendy swallowed a sob and pointed at Juan.

"Juan and me, we went looking for Irene. She never showed up for lunch. We went to her locker first."

Greta nodded reassuringly. "You went to her locker, then what?"

Wendy looked at Juan, then back to Greta. "We walked over to her last class; she wasn't there, the room was empty, we just kept walking. Then we saw something on the ground, over by the bungalows, next to where the cars are parked."

"What?" Greta probed gently, remembering her car was parked there, too. "Was it Irene?"

Wendy rolled her eyes and wailed a piercing, mournful howl. Greta felt chills travel up and down her arms. Juan didn't seem to respond to Wendy's cry at all.

"Try to calm down, Wendy. Take a deep breath and tell us," Greta said.

Wendy swallowed and wiped her nose with her hand. "At first, Juan tried to pick her up. We thought she was just hurt, but when he turned her over, her face . . ."

"Where's Irene?" Greta asked. "What happened to her?"

"Oh, Ms. Gallagher," Wendy choked. "Somebody killed Irene."

12

PONTRELLI tugged at the beefy jowl on the left side of his face. The desk in front of him was sprinkled with powdered sugar and doughnut crumbs. Four empty Styrofoam cups sat in a row beyond the crumbs, one looking as if Pontrelli had taken a little bite out of the rim. He and the crime lab team had been on the campus for hours, searching everywhere, even combing through student lockers and other out-of-the-way corners. The weariness in his eyes told Greta they hadn't found anything except dust and graffiti.

Greta listened to the wind churning the tree branches that were just outside of Adam's office. A large limb, sagging from age, groaned next to the window.

"Let me see if I have this straight," Pontrelli said. "You got about eighteen hundred kids on campus plus all the teachers and other adults. How many does that make?"

Adam looked tortured, his eyes weary and full of remorse. The worst series of incidents ever to take place in the Los Angeles Unified School District, and it had to happen at Adam's school. Greta wanted to put her hand on his, or touch his arm, but she kept a respectable distance. Detective Alice Zamora sat next to Pontrelli, her face stony, indifferent. It was as if a show of rigid formality was her way of separating the law enforcers from the civilians. The walls seemed to be closing in on the four of them.

Adam said, "The teachers and aides plus all the clerical and custodial employees number one hundred and twelve. Then there's the cafeteria staff."

Pontrelli wrote that down. "So we got all these people and nobody sees this girl wandering around by herself having a rendezvous with a murderer."

"Not so far as we know," Adam answered. "The teachers rounded up most of the kids after Irene was discovered and kept them together in the auditorium. A lot of them wouldn't even leave when we dismissed school for the day. They waited around for their parents to pick them up. We've been following emergency dismissal procedures."

"And you say these teachers tried to find us a witness? They talked to every one of those kids?"

"Not exactly," Adam explained. "We don't even have enough seats in the auditorium for the whole student body to convene at one time, but the kids sat on the floor in the aisles or stood in the rear while someone talked to the group over the microphone."

"So who talked to them?"

Greta leaned forward in her chair. "Fran Elliot, the other senior counselor, did at first, then I took over. We begged the kids to tell us anything that might stop this senseless violence, but no one seemed to know anything. Later on, I also talked to Wendy and Juan privately."

Pontrelli looked at his watch, annoyed, like he was late for an appointment with the IRS. "Okay. Let's move on. What was the girl doing way over there in the first place? Don't you have rules about where the kids are supposed to be at lunchtime?"

Greta shook her head. "Technically, Irene was not out of bounds. We have an open campus policy at lunch, and the students can walk around, go to their lockers or a classroom, almost anywhere they want."

"All right," Pontrelli said. "So then, according to the chemistry teacher, Irene asks permission to leave a few minutes early, before the lunch bell. Says it's an emergency, and the teacher didn't even question that?"

"Listen," Adam said, "when a girl goes up to a male teacher and whispers she's got an emergency, we respect her privacy, especially if it's a good student like Irene."

"How do you figure?" Pontrelli asked.

"Because," Greta snapped, "to them, an emergency usually means the girl needs a sanitary napkin, maybe desperately."

Pontrelli didn't exactly blush, but he came close. "They can get away with that excuse to leave class early almost any time they want?"

"No more than once a month," Greta said.

Pontrelli ignored her. "The chemistry teacher says she left the room at about twelve-fifteen. At twelve twenty-one the whole school breaks for lunch, so now you've got kids running loose all over the place."

"For a few minutes," Adam explained, "they go to their lockers and to the rest rooms, but most of them are in the lunch area within about five minutes or so."

"Okay, then at twelve-thirty these two go looking for her— what were their names again?"

"Juan Ballestero and Wendy Yoshimura," Greta said.

Pontrelli checked his notes. "You don't think it's strange that these same two kids were right in the middle of the business last week? I interviewed both of them when the other girl was killed."

"They were all friends," Greta answered.

"Okay," Pontrelli said, "then ten minutes later they find this one, Irene, dead, on the ground next to your car." Pontrelli fixed his eyes on Greta. She half expected him to accuse her Toyota of the crime.

"That's right," she said.

Pontrelli turned to Detective Zamora, who, up until then, had been silently filling another notebook. He stroked his face as if he wanted to see if his beard had grown in the last few minutes.

"I want a list of every adult on campus who doesn't have someone to vouch for his or her whereabouts between twelve-fifteen and twelve-forty."

"Right," Zamora answered.

"And set up some teams to take statements first thing in the morning. I want them to screen these kids in depth. Somebody had to see something."

"Right away." Zamora sprinted out of Adam's office, leaving Greta and Adam alone with Pontrelli.

Adam said, "Do you think it was the same murderer? The same person who killed Belinda?"

"You can come right out and say what you're thinking, Mr. Mason. We've got a kid in Juvenile Hall for murder number one, so it couldn't have been him."

"Are you going to let T.P. go, now that you have another victim?" Greta asked.

"Not so fast," Pontrelli said. "Nobody said it had to be the same perpetrator in both cases."

"You mean there's two different murderers?"

"Happens all the time. Don't you watch TV?"

A jab of pain penetrated Greta's skull. She suspected that the granddaddy of all headaches was working its way up her neck. "What about Rudy Smith? You were going to check him out."

Pontrelli gave her an offhand smirk. "Yeah, I did say that, didn't I? He's got a few priors, but no convictions. Small stuff when he was younger, disorderly conduct, petty theft. He was a punk who decided to get a job, probably figured it was the only way to keep his butt out of jail."

Adam said, "Greta may be right about him. Rudy may have asked Irene to meet him."

Pontrelli studied Adam silently for a moment, then said, "Not likely."

Greta said, "But what if Irene figured out that Rudy killed Belinda? Maybe Rudy murdered Irene to shut her up."

Pontrelli stifled a burp with the back of his hand. "Doesn't look that way. Smith is probably the only one in this whole place who has an ironclad alibi."

"What did he tell you?" Greta asked.

"Nothing. I spoke to your head custodian. He said Smith got permission to leave at eleven forty-five for a dental appointment. He came back at one-fifteen."

"How do you know Rudy made it to the dentist?" she asked. "He could be lying."

"He could be, but the dental office had him signed in at eleven fifty-five."

"Oh," Greta said, but inside she was screaming "Shit!" over and over again. She had been certain Rudy had something to do with both murders, but perhaps it had been only Belinda who had connected with Rudy. "Detective Pontrelli, you said it might be two different murderers."

"Yeah, I said that. You always have to take into account the possibility of a copycat in a case like this. That way one killer takes the rap for both, and the other killer walks. But I'm sensing maybe we got just one perp." Pontrelli looked like he knew a whole lot more than he was telling.

"What makes you suspect only one killer?" Greta asked. She'd give anything for five minutes inside Pontrelli's head. His maddening way of withholding information from them had to be more than police procedure. Pontrelli's little game-playing might explain why he seemed to enjoy the role of interrogator more than his partner did. To Detective Zamora, it was part of the job. To a man like Pontrelli, it was recreation.

Pontrelli stretched his legs and leaned back in his chair. "We'll know more after the lab runs its tests, but we do have death by strangulation in two cases."

Adam said, "But I saw Irene before the police arrived. It was awful the way her face had been beaten."

"From the looks of things, the medical examiner thinks the Flores girl had her face bashed in first, possibly to shut her up, but that didn't kill her."

Dozens of teachers and students had raced to the spot where Irene died, and then immediately regretted what they saw. According to their reports, Irene's lovely young face had taken on the consistency of raw meat. With Irene's blood splattered in all directions, everyone assumed she had been pummeled to death or possibly even stabbed.

"Irene was strangled, too?" Greta asked, trying to conceal the emotion rising in her voice. "How horrible."

"Yeah, this time the killer used a necktie rather than his bare hands."

"A necktie?" Adam said.

Pontrelli nodded. "Crime lab boys found it in a trash can, covered with blood. I can show it to you before I send it on its way to the lab."

Greta massaged the back of her neck with one hand. Would a man be so dumb as to use his own necktie to commit murder? She remembered her first theory. A psycho might do something stupid like that.

"What about T.P.?" she asked. "He certainly didn't kill Irene."

Pontrelli said, "Yeah, I was just about to release him anyway. Of course, we can always pick him up again if necessary, but right now I have a problem with a major bit of circumstantial evidence. Half my case was resting on it." Pontrelli said that about as casually as he might order bacon and eggs over easy for breakfast.

"Why didn't you tell us you were going to release T.P.?" Greta fairly shouted.

"I was busy. I had to get the facts on this new case, remember."

"What bit of evidence are you talking about?" Adam asked.

"Well . . ." Pontrelli began.

He was going to drag this out for an eternity. Greta's temples pounded in rhythm with the wind stroking the tree branches against the windowpane.

Pontrelli finally continued. "The crime lab did a DNA typing on the Jackson girl and the fetal tissue. We had to get all kinds of releases just to do a blood sample on the boy. The laws that protect juveniles in custody are enough to tie both your hands behind your back."

"What would a blood sample on the boy prove?" Greta asked.

"Whether or not he matched the fetal DNA. Whether or not he could possibly have fathered the dead girl's baby. We've been working up a case that hinged on him being the father."

"And?" Greta held her breath.

"We got an exclusion on the test. No way on earth could T.P. Bench be the father of the Jackson girl's baby."

13

GRETA watched a smug look unfurl over Pontrelli's broad face. Pontrelli had planned to release T.P. all along, but he withheld that little bit of information until he was ready to leave campus. It was almost perverse. The old buzzard enjoyed aggravating them. What did he do for entertainment on his days off? Rip wings off houseflies?

Pontrelli got up from the chair and walked stiff-legged over to the window. "I see the boys from the lab just pulled up in front of the school, so why don't we walk out to the van and take a look at that necktie?"

Greta and Adam followed Pontrelli to the visitors' parking lot in front of the administration building. Behind the police line, a group of kids and adults stood vigil on the sidewalk. They didn't seem to be talking to one another, just watching silently from a distance as the crime scene workers came and went. From this remote location, there was little to see, since Irene had been found halfway across campus, but the spectators seemed content merely to view the crime scene vehicle, a plain blue-and-white van, up close.

Pontrelli talked to two men inside the van for a minute, then one of the men produced a plastic bag from a big box. Inside the bag, a rather gaudy blue-and-green necktie with dark brown stains curled against the plastic. Greta recognized it at once.

"This looks like the murder weapon, but tests will confirm that, of course," Pontrelli said. "Either of you ever see this before?"

"No, I don't think so," Adam said. "You recognize it?" he asked Greta.

"Well, I'm not certain, it's hard to see, stuffed in a bag like that, but it does look like a tie I saw Stanley Deep wearing yesterday or maybe it was last Friday. I'm not sure."

"Deep's one of your teachers, right?"

"Yes," Adam answered. "Math. Algebra and Geometry."

Greta's heart sank. How could Stanley be involved in Irene's murder? Stanley was a pain in the ass most of the time, but he was really a pretty decent fellow when you cut through the crap of his coming on to every woman he knew. Greta suspected Stanley was probably the most insecure person she had ever met, and his Don Juan routine was a pathetic attempt to cover up his inadequacies, especially concerning his ability to relate to women. She hoped she was wrong about the tie, but she couldn't think of another person who would have the gall to buy such a tie, let alone wear it. But then a more logical thought took hold. What if Rudy had figured out a way to get his hands on one of Stanley's ties?

Pontrelli said, "Well, I guess we'll have to talk to Mr. Deep about his neckties, won't we? Oh, and there's one other thing, Mr. Mason."

"Yes?"

Pontrelli said something under his breath to the man guarding the large box, and the tie was now shifted to a different, smaller box. "A lot of people are getting nervous about all this. There's talk going on between the community relations people over at Foothill Division and the board of education."

"What kind of talk?"

"Talk about shutting down this school until things cool off. No decisions have been made yet, at least not as far as I know. I just thought you should be prepared."

Adam's lower jaw slacked open for a second. Even after he recovered and spoke, his eyes betrayed his anxiety. "I don't suppose there's any way we can stay open?"

"None that I can see, but, of course, it's not up to me. What with the public yelling and screaming, I think the board would be foolish to press to stay open."

"What about the crisis center we've set up? Greta and the other counselors are working overtime, helping these kids handle their grief."

Pontrelli's eyes locked onto Adam's. "I don't know anything about that. We just don't want to find another dead body on this campus."

Individual schools were closed only under the most severe circumstances. Greta remembered the time they had carried on as usual with a brush fire raging over the mountain terrain to the north. Unless it appeared the school itself was about to ignite, school was in session. Pontrelli sounded more than cautious. The police department probably thought this crime spree was not going to end with two murders.

"Detective Pontrelli," Greta said, "I was wondering if, by any chance, you remember the name of Rudy Smith's dentist?"

He jerked his head toward her, a quizzical look on his face. "Why, you got a toothache?"

Greta wished she had one of Stanley's neckties to twist around Pontrelli's neck. "No, but I've been thinking."

Pontrelli sighed. "Let's have it."

"Well," she went on, noticing Adam cringe slightly, "his appointment took him off campus for an hour and a half. It takes me a half hour just to get to my dentist. I was wondering how far he had to drive."

Pontrelli flipped open his little notebook. "Smith went to the family clinic run by a Dr. Ortiz right over on Foothill Boulevard. From here, my guess is it would take him about five minutes on that little Yamaha of his."

"Oh," she said, "you already thought of that."

"Yes, Mrs. Gallagher, I thought of that. You got anything else bothering you?"

Greta felt the color rise in her face, but she was not sorry she had given Pontrelli a chance to embarrass her. Perhaps she could do Pontrelli's job a bit more efficiently than he could. Just knowing Rudy had arrived at the clinic wasn't enough. Rudy was devious. It would be just like him to set himself up with an alibi. It wouldn't hurt to check it out.

Pontrelli waved the van on its way to the lab, and he started for the unmarked brown Plymouth sedan parked off to the left. "We're gonna go over this place again tomorrow, and I want to talk to every adult who works on this campus. You think you can set that up?"

"Of course," Adam answered quickly. "Anything I can do to help."

"Does this mean you now think a school employee killed both girls?" Greta asked.

Pontrelli almost smiled. "That's one angle, but I still have our young friend Juan Ballestero pretty high on my list of suspects."

"Juan was taken to the hospital, wasn't he? He was in shock. He barely made sense when I talked to him," Greta said.

"We'll see. Maybe he's been released from the hospital. Maybe he's studying to be an actor. Maybe he put on a show for the benefit of a very large audience." With that, Pontrelli was in the car, the ignition grinding as he cranked the key. He drove away.

"Pontrelli is the most infuriating individual I have ever met in my entire life," Greta said to the rear of the detective's car.

She turned to Adam. "He's going to harass Juan just like he persecuted T.P. You could tell Juan wasn't acting, couldn't you?"

Adam took her elbow and directed her back through the main gate. Putting his arm around her would be inappropriate on school grounds, but elbow directing seemed protective rather than affectionate. What she wanted from Adam right now was a hug.

"I thought Juan was horrified by what he saw. I know I was," Adam answered as they walked.

"I'm glad I didn't see Irene's face, all beaten and bloody. Finding Belinda was bad enough."

"I know. I hope Pontrelli wraps this up quickly."

Greta studied his face. "Are you all right?"

Adam forced a wan smile. "Sure, considering my credibility as a principal just went out to sea. Maybe the superintendent will find a nice little job for me somewhere counting pencils and paper clips."

"You don't think they'll actually demote you because of this, do you? It isn't your fault."

"Greta, look at it from a parent's point of view. A girl is killed in cold blood right under our noses. Where was our supervision? Why wasn't somebody over there keeping an eye on things?"

"It's not like these parents keep an eye on their teenagers all day long. They don't know where their kids are eighty percent of the time."

Adam shook his head. "It doesn't matter. Kids are supposed to be safe in a school. When they're not, somebody's head has to roll."

"You can fight it. Let a court decide whether the random act of another person was the result of your negligence. It'll never stick."

"Well, the least I can expect is a transfer to another school.

Probably down to the south-central area, as far away from McCormick High as they can get. The worst part is I'll miss seeing you every day."

"So you'll fight a transfer. Don't let the board push you around."

"It doesn't work that way. Remember, I'm not protected by your union, and the board has to answer to the community. They'll move me just to quiet things down. The community will see the board taking action against me and that will probably satisfy them."

Greta's mouth went dry. Adam was right. The board of education would have to "attend" to a principal whose students were murdered at high noon on campus.

They walked slowly, in silence, heading toward the bungalows and the place where Greta had left her car, the same spot where Irene had been found. It was almost dark now. The day had faded into a fiery sunset, and now that the sun was almost gone, the wind gave up its collision course with every stray piece of debris on campus and simply stopped. The air was cool, clotting about them with a sudden, unfamiliar dampness.

They turned the corner at the rear of the auditorium and walked into a TV news team taping a report. They tried to duck inside the building, but the crew was too fast for them. A tall man with a flawlessly smooth haircut, somewhat resembling a helmet, bounded toward them.

"Excuse me, sir, could we have your reaction to what has happened here today?"

Adam stepped up to the microphone the man thrust at him. "We're all saddened and shocked that such a dreadful incident could have taken place in our school. All of us at McCormick extend our deepest sympathies to the family of Irene Flores. She was a shining example of a student, a delightful girl who was loved by all her friends and teachers."

Adam's voice cracked on the last sentence, but the camera

kept rolling. Greta thought Adam's speech had sounded a little canned, direct from some guidebook for principals put out by the board of education. What a shame, since she knew his emotions were genuine. Adam cared about their students; he deplored what was happening at McCormick. Finally, when Adam regained his composure, another man, who had been following behind the camera, waved for the filming to stop.

The man with the microphone called out, "Good one. Get his name and position."

While Adam reported his name, rank, and serial number, Greta realized her headache was back. Perhaps it had never left. A dull ache across her neck and shoulders confirmed that she was tired and tense, and dodging reporters didn't help. She expected the microphone in her face next, but the news team had apparently lost interest. All at once, like a single organism sharing a primitive brain, they began to move toward the gate.

"I hope that's the last bunch of reporters for today," Greta said. "They really don't help."

"No, but for a country that lives on television, they're important. People thrive on tragedy."

They walked past the quad, a large grassy area in the dead center of the campus. Lawn sprinklers twirled in the near darkness, fanning water onto the paved walk.

"Adam, how smart do you think Rudy Smith really is?"

"Not smart enough to fool a dentist into thinking he filled his teeth when he didn't."

"How did you know that's what I was leading up to?"

He grinned. "I don't know. I get the feeling you're not done with your detective work even though I've asked you to stay out of it, for your sake."

"I'm not really doing anything. Just throwing ideas at Pontrelli."

"Well, I guess Pontrelli doesn't mind a little help, but I also suspect he can handle the job on his own."

They reached the parking area between the bungalows. All the cars were gone except for Greta's Toyota and one last police vehicle. The yellow police warning line had been tied through the handle of her door. On the ground, a white tape outline of the fallen Irene picked up the reflection of an exterior light and glared back at them.

Adam reeled her around and pulled her away from the car. "You don't need to get entangled in this. You've been through enough for one day. I'll drive you home tonight, and we'll get your car out of here tomorrow."

"How will I get to work tomorrow?"

Adam looked at her. "I'll be at your door to pick you up first thing in the morning, unless you agree to let me spend the night."

14

"HOLY shit!" Maxine yanked a paper towel from the wall dispenser in the ladies' rest room, sending a clatter of silvery bracelets tumbling from her wrist almost to her elbow. "I don't believe you actually did it. You slept with a fucking principal?"

"Not so loud, for God's sake," Greta said. "I hadn't planned to tell the whole school."

"You slept with a fucking principal," Maxine said again, this time in a whisper. She looked at Greta, her brow wrinkled. "No pun intended."

"Will you stop making a federal case out of it? I'm sorry I told you."

"Okay, okay, I'm sorry. Shoot me, already, but what did you expect me to say? 'Oh, really, darling, you had our principal, dear Adam, spend the night. How terribly clever of you.'" Maxine ran a tiny comb through her eyebrows. "I hope you practiced safe sex. You never know what a principal might be carrying."

"Knock it off, Maxine. I mean it."

"All right. So how was he? I can't imagine a principal being worth the trouble."

"Well, you're wrong. He . . . it was wonderful."

"Details. I need details. Tell me everything."

"That can wait. I need a favor—"

"Favors can wait," Maxine said. "Tell me how he measured up, literally."

"Max, just shut up for a minute and listen to me, will you? I need you to cover for me during your free period."

Maxine's eyes grew wide. "Cover, for what? What in hell are you up to?" Then a sudden understanding crept across her face. "Don't tell me you two are off to a little matinee in the supply room?"

Greta let out a deep breath. "Don't be stupid. This has nothing to do with Adam, except that I don't want him to know I'm going off campus for a few minutes this morning."

Maxine gazed at the mirror over the sink, fluffing her hair with her fingers. "I don't suppose you're going to tell me where you're sneaking off to?"

"Later. Just be in the auditorium at the beginning of period two. Adam plans to parade every kid who shows up today past the police, alphabetically—"

"You're kidding. That ought to send them over the nearest fence. You honestly think they'll just wait around so you can walk them through a lineup?"

Greta dabbed another coat of lipstick over her already pink lips. "It won't be a lineup. That's the best way we could think of to screen the kids without running into a lot of duplication. We'll start with the A's in period one and just summon the kids letter by letter over the PA system."

"Amazing what you two can come up with when you put your heads together."

"Listen, the counselors and any teacher who has a free period will have to report to the aud to help out until we get through this."

Maxine fussed with the little wisps of hair tousled across her forehead.

Greta caught Maxine's eye in the mirror. "Adam will make an announcement explaining the procedure right after the first bell. You have to be there anyway, so just say I went for an aspirin or something if Adam or Pontrelli asks where I am. That's all I'm asking, okay?"

"Sure, why not? But if I cover for you, you've got to give me a detailed report on last night's little romp with ol' Adam. I want it all. Blow by blow."

Greta grinned. "I should have my head examined for telling you anything."

Maxine pushed open the door to the corridor. Pontrelli stood right across the hall talking to Adam.

"I'm off to my class," Maxine said. "Looks like Kojak is ready to turn this place into Devil's Island."

Greta walked over to Adam. Even though he had driven her to school not more than fifteen minutes earlier, the flesh on the back of her neck tingled when their eyes met. Was her shiver noticeable? She had told Maxine about her first intimacy with Adam simply because she couldn't contain her joy another second. She had to tell someone. Maxine would probably rant and rave until Greta told her at least one or two details, but Greta wanted to safeguard the highlights of their lovemaking. What she had going with Adam was just too special to share.

Now she wondered if Pontrelli could read her face. Did he know she and Adam had fallen into bed so greedy for each other that, for a time at least, even the two murders had been forgotten?

Adam's face lit up when he saw her. His smile triggered something inside her gut to do a little dance against her solar plexus.

Adam said, "We're going to walk over to Stanley's room. Detective Pontrelli wants to talk to him before his students arrive."

Greta had almost forgotten about Stanley's necktie. Since she'd awakened this morning with Adam sleeping at her side, she'd almost forgotten her own name. "Mind if I tag along?"

Pontrelli said, "Good idea. You're the one that identified the tie. Lead the way."

They crossed the open lunch area on the way to room 26. A group of scraggly pigeons pecked away at fallen crumbs, hardly stopping to move out of the way of the intruders. Greta stepped around a particularly stubborn brown pigeon who was working his way through a discarded scrap of bread.

The aroma of frying bacon and fresh-baked sweet rolls drifted toward them, but only a handful of students sat at the tables eating the free breakfast provided for them by a federal program. They'd be lucky if one third of the student body showed up for school the day after Irene's death. They'd be even luckier if they managed to pull together any semblance of real education during this entire school year.

The door to room 26 stood open and Stanley sat at the teacher's desk sipping coffee from a stained mug. Greta could smell the coffee as they entered the room. Stanley looked up. A smile began to cross his lips, but when Stanley spotted Pontrelli, the welcoming smile disappeared.

Without wasting time on small talk, Pontrelli pulled the plastic bag containing the bloodstained necktie from his inside jacket pocket.

"I've been told this necktie might belong to you," Pontrelli said, dangling the bag between his thumb and forefinger. "You recognize it?"

Stanley stood up slowly, squinting at the soiled necktie through the plastic. He reached for his glasses, then walked closer. Greta knew Stanley was only in his forties, but suddenly he appeared frail, like an old man.

"Dang, it sure looks like one of mine. Let's check." Stanley walked around them, past the rows of student chairs to the rear of the room. He opened the narrow cupboard that served as the teacher's coat closet in each of the classrooms. On the inside of the door, hanging from a hook, about a dozen or more garishly ugly neckties glared at them. One especially offensive tie had repetitive bright yellow fish with their open mouths ready to clamp down on a fisherman's lure.

Stanley rummaged through the ties, shaking his head. "Last time I wore it, I'm sure I left it right here, with the others. I usually take off my tie by fifth period when it gets too warm in the room."

Pontrelli fingered the neckwear. He handled Stanley's ties carefully, as if poor taste was something that could rub off and leave a stain on your hands. "You keep all your ties here, at school?"

Stanley grinned. "Just my work ties. I have the good ones at home."

"You keep this closet locked?" Pontrelli asked.

"I lost the key years ago, and I never bothered to replace it. There's nothing valuable inside, just my ties."

"Anybody else know where you keep your ties?" Pontrelli looked like he was fighting off an urge to pop Stanley on the nose, and Greta did her best not to show her delight. Stanley wasn't capable of organizing his wardrobe, let alone a series of murders.

"Sure," Stanley said, "all my students know where I keep them. The boys often borrow my ties. I guess when they want to impress a lady."

Greta winced. She could visualize a kid borrowing one of his hideous neckties, then making an ass out of Stanley by imitating him in front of a locker room full of howling boys. Sometimes kids could be very cruel.

Pontrelli seemed to be fuming inside as they marched toward the auditorium. His only real lead in Irene's case wasn't much of a lead after all.

"Okay," Pontrelli barked at Adam, "let's see if your plan to interview the students gives us anything to go on. We damn well better come up with something pretty soon."

Detective Zamora was already in the auditorium, ordering around several other police officers and the counselors and teachers who were there to assist with the first round of questioning. Greta noticed that Zamora retreated to the sidelines the minute Pontrelli stomped into the room. She was thankful she worked for someone as gentle as Adam rather than a brute like Pontrelli.

After the call went out over the public address system for teachers to send all students whose last names began with the letter A to the auditorium, about forty kids paraded into the building. It seemed the students fell into two categories: those too terrified to come anywhere near McCormick High and those who knew nothing about the crime but wanted desperately to be in the middle of the investigation. Maybe a third category, someone who had actually witnessed Rudy Smith luring Irene to the spot where she died, would dare to speak out.

By the beginning of second period, they had worked through the A's, B's, and C's. No one had seen a thing. Maxine walked into the auditorium and nodded almost imperceptibly at Greta.

Greta headed for the rear door of the auditorium and slipped outside. The D's were already filing toward the building. Greta greeted a few of them but kept walking. She wasn't far from the bungalows, but each step seemed like a mile. If the police had removed their yellow warning tape from her car, the rest would be easy.

Her Toyota sat in the space between the bungalows all by itself. The police tape was gone. Even the teachers who usually parked there had been cautious today. Greta guessed that if the choice was between vandalism and murder, vandalism wasn't such a bad choice. Her hand trembled slightly when she unlocked the door, but she was certain she'd made it to the car without attracting attention. She slid behind the wheel and closed the door. She checked the rearview mirror and the black-top in front of her. No one was around.

The engine sputtered, then started on the second try. She eased the car away from the bungalows toward the service drive. So far so good.

Now if she could only convince Dr. Ortiz she had a right to review Rudy Smith's dental records, her mission would be a success.

15

WHEN she reached the gate, Greta turned left, taking what everyone called "the back way" to Foothill Boulevard. By taking the less-traveled streets, she might avoid running into anyone who might recognize her. God, now she was beginning to think like some two-bit detective who tracked unfaithful husbands and their lovers to cheap motels.

This section of the San Fernando Valley had never been built up the way her own neighborhood fifteen miles south had grown. Here there were open spaces between houses, zoning that permitted horses, and many litter-strewn vacant lots still waiting for the bite of a developer's bulldozer. She had driven these streets for twelve years, but she still felt like an outsider, a stranger in a small town, whenever she ventured beyond the high school campus.

Pontrelli had guessed right about the time it took to get to the dental clinic. In five minutes, she saw the sign.

She pulled into one of three parking spaces directly in front of the Ortiz Family Dental Clinic. She stretched her arms out fully, squeezing the steering wheel until her back pressed hard against the seat of the car. What was she doing here? She turned off the ignition, wondering how she could screw up enough courage to actually go inside the place. Maybe this was why detectives in the movies drank so much.

This whole idea was crazy. Whatever made her think she could pull off impersonating a school official? Maybe what she was about to do was even illegal. Pontrelli would probably hit the ceiling. He could also make waves with the school district that could cost her plenty.

But, more important than that, what if her scheme didn't work? Adam would be furious. Come to think of it, he might be furious even if it *did* work, even if she was doing her best to protect him from a transfer to God knows where. After last night with Adam, she didn't want to be the one to shatter the afterglow, not after waiting so long for the warm, fuzzy feeling that lolled inside her head.

But she mustn't forget Belinda and Irene. She had to do whatever she could to find their killer, and she had made it this far. She grabbed her purse and went inside.

The waiting room was shabby and poorly lit. Cheap plastic-covered chairs lined the walls. The chairs looked wobbly and the vinyl looked sticky. Stacks of rumpled magazines leaned at odd angles on a small table in one corner. Across the room, a dark-eyed woman struggled to keep a small boy and an even smaller baby from wriggling off her lap. She hissed something in Spanish to the children and avoided Greta's eyes.

The air hung heavy with the sharp smell of medicinal odors. A woman sat in a little office behind a sliding window in the far wall of the waiting room. She didn't look up.

Greta reached inside her wallet, withdrawing two cards. She carefully positioned her district employee identification card so it overlapped another card, her faculty pass to McCormick High activities. The bottom card revealed only her photo on the left side and MCCORMICK HIGH at the top. Greta approached the sliding window and held up both cards, trying desperately to steady her hand.

The woman raised her eyelids first and then her chin. Good.

She wore bifocals. Reading the small print from this distance would not be easy.

The woman slid the rattling pane of glass to one side. "May I help you?"

Greta quickly tucked her identification inside her purse. Her hands trembled slightly; her armpits felt damp. "Yes, I hope so. I have to discuss a rather delicate issue. It concerns one of McCormick High School's employees taking time off from his job, claiming he received treatment here when we believe he was elsewhere."

The woman glanced over her shoulder. The whirring grind of a dentist's drill came from one of the three examination rooms behind her. "Maybe you'd better step in here," she said, motioning to the door at Greta's left. The woman closed the sliding window with a series of tiny lurches.

Greta entered the inner office and pulled the door shut. From this vantage point, she looked down on the woman's desk. A clutter of paperwork and insurance forms hinted that the woman headed a clerical staff of one. If she could get what she wanted from the receptionist, so much the better. She wasn't sure she could fool the dentist with her story.

"Now," the woman said, "I'm not exactly sure what we can do to help you."

Greta shot a sideways glance through the window, checking to see if anyone else had entered the waiting room. The mother continued to juggle her two children, wearing the baby around her neck while trying to calm the older child into waiting patiently. A loud squawk from the baby reached the inner office.

"I believe you were questioned yesterday, by the police, about an appointment one of our employees claimed he had with Dr. Ortiz." Greta lowered her voice. "Rudy Smith."

The woman perked up. "Oh, yes, I checked on that myself." She hesitated a moment, then said, "You don't mean to tell me the police suspect Mr. Smith . . . He didn't have anything to do with that awful business I heard about on the news last night, did he?"

Greta stood ramrod straight. "I'm not at liberty to discuss the case, but we do need to know exactly how long Mr. Smith was here. You claim he signed in at eleven fifty-five A.M."

The woman shuffled through the mountain of papers on the left side of her desk. She produced a lined yellow legal notepad covered with handwritten signatures. "Yes, the detective who was here, a lady, said I should hang on to this."

Zamora, Greta thought.

"See, right here's his name, which he signed. I filled in the time in the first column, eleven fifty-five."

"Yes, that much we know, but now we need to know when he left. How long did his dental work take?" Greta pursed her lips, trying to emphasize with her expression just how critical the woman's help would be.

The woman blanched. "For that, I'd have to check his dental records."

"Yes, if you don't mind. We really appreciate your help. You see, we're trying to keep things very quiet. You know how hysterical people can become."

"Yes, I know what you mean." The woman stood. "My niece and nephew went to McCormick High a few years back. Perhaps you remember them, Jorge and Yolanda Reyes?"

"Yes, of course," Greta lied. She might remember their faces, but the names became a blur after a year or so. "Both good students, as I recall."

The woman smiled. "Let me just take a look at his file. You do understand I can't let you remove any records from this office."

"Of course," Greta answered. "If Detective Zamora needs the doctor's files, she'll subpoena them through the proper channels, I assure you."

The sound of the dentist's drill had stopped. Greta heard voices and the clatter of instruments. Hurry, please, hurry, she urged the woman via mental telepathy. The woman slowly paged through dog-eared folders in an open file drawer.

"Here it is." She began to read. "That's funny."

Greta's pulse quickened. "What's funny? Did he have an appointment yesterday?"

"Well, yes, Rudy Smith saw the doctor. Now that I think of it, I remember Doctor's assistant calling his name, so he went into one of the exam rooms all right."

Greta's hands fisted at her sides. She had stuck her neck out for nothing. "Can you estimate how long his appointment lasted?"

"Well, normally I could, but according to what the doctor wrote here, he was in and right out again."

Greta strained to read the file across the desk. The woman's finger followed the handwritten scrawl. "We'll have to ask the doctor just how long he was in there."

"No need to bother him if he's with a patient," Greta said quickly. "What did the doctor write?"

The woman shrugged. "Says right here, 'patient will reschedule,' then there's this little symbol we use." The woman pointed.

Greta breathed deeply, trying to control the steady thumping of her heart. She had to get out of here. Her knees had turned liquid, and she was afraid she was going to hyperventilate. "What exactly does the little symbol mean?"

"It means I'm not to bill the patient. In other words, the doctor may have talked to Mr. Smith for a few minutes, but he didn't spend enough time with him to perform a billable procedure."

16

GRETA sped back to the high school not caring if anyone recognized her or even if she ran a red light. Rudy Smith was the killer. His little charade had given him at least an hour to sneak back on campus, murder Irene, leave for the second time, then return again a half hour after the body had been discovered. Not a bad piece of work for a little sleaze like Rudy, but not good enough either.

This time Greta parked in the regular faculty lot next to the library. Now there were two spots on campus she wanted to avoid. Second period would be over soon, so she rushed toward the auditorium.

"You all right?" a voice came from behind.

Greta jumped, certain her feet had left the ground. God, she was a nervous wreck. She turned slowly. It was Adam. "Hi, yes," she stammered. "Why wouldn't I be all right?"

"Maxine said you went to take an aspirin and lie down for a little while. I missed you."

"Oh, yes." She didn't want to take time to explain her cover-up story at the moment. It was just a little lie, and she had to get Pontrelli on Rudy Smith's tail right away. "Where's Detective Pontrelli?"

Adam moved closer to her. She could smell his after-shave. Damn stuff drove her crazy.

"He's interviewing teachers in the conference room. Why?"

"I'll explain it to you when I explain it to him. Let's just say I've got good news."

Adam's expression was hard to read. Somewhere between confusion and a touch of hurt feelings, she guessed. "Just trust me until we find Pontrelli."

Adam walked next to her, but he didn't speak again until they reached the conference room. He covered her hand with his own when she reached out to knock on the door. "Darling, what have you been up to? Tell me before we go inside."

His endearment was too much. She wanted to drag him into the nurse's office across the hall where they could find a cot. Hell, she didn't even need a cot. She couldn't remember being this horny since the tenth grade.

"All right," she gave in, "I'll tell you, but promise to hear me out before you say a word."

"Sure."

Greta didn't know where to begin. Maybe it would be best to cut to the bottom line and simply start with the fact that Rudy had lied to the police and the head custodian. Adam's eyes locked onto hers. God, he was gorgeous. Before she had a chance to begin her story, however, the conference room door swung open and Cecelia Hartman pushed into the hall, stepping directly between them. Cecelia shook herself slightly and drew her square shoulders up close to her ears, giving her the look of a bulldog, that is if you could find a bulldog with a flounce of lace at the collar.

Cecelia said, "I, for one, will be very happy when this school returns to normal. Adam, do you realize I had exactly two pupils in my first period class, and none in period two?" Cecelia finally noticed Greta. "Oh, hello, Greta."

"Hi," Greta said.

Pontrelli stepped into the doorway behind Cecelia. "Oh, it's you, Mr. Mason. Miss Hartman here was just explaining to me how her academic schedule has been disrupted by this nasty police business."

Adam tried not to smile. He covered his mouth with his hand and coughed.

Greta said, "Detective Pontrelli, could I speak to you for a moment? It's very important."

Cecelia fired a dirty look in Greta's direction. Greta hadn't meant that Cecelia's problem was unimportant, but . . . Hell, there was no point in trying to apologize to Cecelia. Cecelia turned on her size-nine double narrows and stamped down the hall.

Greta followed Adam and Pontrelli into the conference room and closed the door. "I didn't mean to upset Cecelia, but I've got news that can't wait."

Adam pulled out a chair for her to sit. "Don't worry about Cecelia. In ten minutes she'll find someone else to be upset with and she'll forget all about you. Now what's this very important news you have?"

Pontrelli looked as if his thoughts were a million miles away, but by now Greta had learned he was accurately recording every word she said. Adam gazed at her, his eyes filled with tenderness, but by the time she had recounted the details of her visit to the dental clinic, his expression turned sullen, almost on the verge of bad-tempered.

At first Pontrelli simply grunted and fidgeted with his ballpoint pen. The pen looked as if it were about to snap in two.

Greta said, "Detective Pontrelli, I hope you're not angry I cut into your territory. I just knew Rudy was not to be trusted, and I had to find out for myself."

Adam stood up and began to pace. "Well, I don't know if Detective Pontrelli is upset, but I sure am. Greta, this is not like you, to go running about like some undercover cop, when you have duties right here on campus. If word of this ever gets downtown, your job, at least your counseling job, could be on the line."

Pontrelli's face was so red Greta fully expected to see little puffs of steam burst from his ears. Finally, Pontrelli said, "I don't give a rat's ass about your position. I just hope you haven't compromised any of the evidence in this investigation with your snooping. There are laws against impersonating a police officer, you know."

"I was not impersonating a police officer," Greta said. "I was impersonating a school official."

Pontrelli's face got a little redder. He turned to Adam. "Can you find someone out there to fetch Detective Zamora for me?"

"Sure." Adam hurried into the main office.

Pontrelli turned back to Greta. "I'll make you a deal. You let me do my job the way I've been trained, and I promise I won't try to teach any of your classes."

Something inside Greta's brain exploded. "Dammit, you're not being fair. I asked the questions Detective Zamora should have asked. What time Rudy Smith left the dentist's office is crucial. And don't forget this is the first real lead you've had in this case."

A desire to kill seemed to pulse in Pontrelli's eyes. Adam walked in, flashing a glance between Pontrelli and Greta. "Detective Zamora is on her way."

"Thanks," Pontrelli said.

Adam looked at Greta, but spoke to Pontrelli. "Don't be too rough on her. I'm sure she was just trying to help. As long as downtown doesn't find out she was pretending to act in an official capacity, I guess it'll be all right."

Pontrelli shook his head. "Yeah, I'm sure everything will be just peachy."

A wave of gratitude washed over Greta. As upset as he was,

Adam had stuck up for her. She looked directly at Adam. "I won't do anything like that again."

"Good," Adam said, smiling slightly. "Frankly, I'm surprised that dentist's receptionist gave you any information at all."

Pontrelli glared at Greta. "Oh, I don't know. It's amazing how people respond to the flash of a badge, isn't it, Mrs. Gallagher?"

The door behind them opened. The principal's secretary stuck her head into the room. "Excuse me, Mr. Mason, but there's something you should see."

"Come on in, Connie," Adam said.

Connie tiptoed into the room. Connie didn't look much like a secretary. Her tight cotton dress would have been better suited for a trip to the laundromat, but there was no question about her efficiency. "I collected the mail from your box," Connie said to Adam, "and this was in an envelope that had no writing on the outside." She handed him a piece of notebook paper with three holes punched along one side.

As if she had suddenly become aware of her short, stubby fingernails, Connie hid her hands behind her back. She said, "It seemed unusual, and Detective Pontrelli said to let you or him know if I noticed anything unusual."

"Thank you, Connie. You were absolutely right." Adam studied the piece of paper.

"What is it?" Pontrelli asked.

"I guess you could call it a letter of resignation. Or maybe two words of resignation."

Adam tossed the single sheet onto the table. Greta and Pontrelli read together. "I quit. Signed, Rudy Smith."

17

PONTRELLI swallowed the last of the coffee in his cup. The scowl on his face told Greta it probably tasted god-awful. He pushed away from the table and stood, hiking his pants up around his waist.

"I guess we need to pull in Mr. Smith for questioning." He walked out into the main office and picked up the phone.

Greta got up from her chair and faced Adam. "I'm sorry. I didn't mean to upset you, but I've had this feeling, ever since Rudy left his fingerprint on Belinda's program card, that he was the one."

Adam kept an eye on Pontrelli through the open door for a few moments, then walked over and gave the door a push hard enough to close it. Greta rushed into his arms.

"It's all right," he said, pulling back just far enough so he could face her. He smiled, melting her fear. "I could never stay angry with you, at least not for very long." He kissed her lightly, then released his hold on her.

Thank God he understood. Perhaps he didn't like the idea of her being a snoop. Most men hated nosy women, but what she had done was different, wasn't it? A little bit of detective work did not fall into the same category.

"When they find Rudy," she said, "this nightmare will be over, and McCormick will return to normal."

He walked back over to the window. "I hope so."

Greta felt an outpouring of love for Adam, and all of her vows never to consider a second marriage suddenly evaporated.

She said, "Will I see you tonight?"

He turned to face her. The worry—or was it frustration?—veiling his face vanished as he smiled. "I'm surprised you feel you have to ask."

"Well, I didn't know if you had other—"

He reached out and placed his forefinger over her lips. "I have no other plans, no other dates, no other desires. If that's okay with you."

"I don't have any problem with that arrangement."

"You'll be seeing so much of me, you'll probably want to run for cover. I love you, Greta."

Tears rose in the corners of her eyes. "Everything has happened so fast. I wasn't sure at first, but now I know. I love you, too, Adam."

He took her hand and kissed it. First the back of her hand, then he turned it over and kissed her palm. "We do have to be somewhat circumspect here at school, you know."

Her hand would probably tingle for the rest of her life. "I know, it's all right. I can wait."

Adam laughed out loud. "Then you're doing better than me. Right now I'd like nothing more than to rip your clothes off and make love to you right on top of the conference table."

Who would have guessed she could become sexually aroused this close to a mimeograph machine? "Maybe I'd better get out of here. I'll go see if they need my help in the aud."

"I'll see you later."

Greta walked into the main office aware that she had a wide grin stuck on her face. The bell jangled her back to reality. So much had happened in the last hour, it hadn't all fully registered. She grabbed a stack of mail from her mailbox and tried to shuffle it into a neater, more manageable pile as she strolled away.

"There you are," Maxine scolded. "Where in hell have you been?"

"On cloud nine."

"Oh, fuck. You get one piece of ass and your mind turns to slop. C'mon." Maxine looped her arm through Greta's and dragged her out of the office into the corridor. "Walk me to my classroom. Who knows—I might even have one kid waiting for class."

"How'd it go in the auditorium?" Greta asked.

"The kids have spread the word. Half of them were over the fence or out the back gate before we got ten minutes into period two. It's hopeless. They don't want to go through this question-answer bullshit, and I don't blame them."

Maxine was right. It was passing period between two and three, but the campus was practically empty. Across the quad, a few teachers walked toward the auditorium, their footsteps echoing in a hollow, mismatched patter, and the newly expanded army of school security officers patrolled in pairs, but most of the kids had disappeared.

She hoped the kids had enough sense to go straight home. This was not the time to be drinking beer and smoking cigarettes—or worse—in a vacant lot somewhere. No telling what drove Rudy to do what he had done so far. Greta prayed that when Rudy was safely locked up somewhere the students would settle down—and even Cecelia's academic schedule could return to its usual rut.

Maxine unlocked the door to her classroom. The odor of drying papier-mâché drifted outside. "Look at this. Not one kid in sight. How am I supposed to run an art program with no artists?"

"I've never seen the campus look so barren," Greta said.

"Schools are kind of creepy without kids. Did the tardy bell ring?"

The tardy bell answered for itself.

"See, I told you. It'll be days before we see kids around this place again. Now are you going to tell me where you've been, or do I have to throttle it out of you?"

"I guess I can tell you now. They won't need me in the aud if there aren't any kids to interview."

Maxine turned on the lights in the room and propped open both doors. A gentle breeze lessened the heavy odor of the drying paper. The wet projects sat on a table in the rear of the room, and although they were still in a very early stage, Greta knew they would somehow evolve into the colorful piñatas so popular with all the students.

Greta went through her story again. Maxine interrupted every few words, inching to the very edge of the chair she had placed directly in front of Greta's.

"So Pontrelli was really pissed?" Maxine asked.

" 'Pissed' is putting it mildly. He got so angry his earlobes turned purple."

"Then what?"

Greta told her about Rudy's sudden resignation, then paused.

Maxine bounced a little, excited, like a child who couldn't wait to hear good news. "There's more. I can tell there's more."

Greta confided that Adam had said he loved her. She even told Maxine the part about Adam wanting to make love on the conference room table.

"Hot damn. So good ol' Adam turns out to be an animal after all." Maxine slapped her knee and settled back in her chair. "So what's next?"

"What do you mean?"

"Well, it's no secret you've got the hots for one another, but is that it? You working this up into one sensational affair, or have you set your sights higher? I'd hate to see you get hurt, you know."

"I know you're the expert on men and sex, but I'm not sure I'm following your line of thought," Greta said.

"Listen up, Grets. Adam wants to jump your bones and you're not exactly interested in fighting him off, but that's probably as far as it's going to go. Don't start getting all moony-eyed about orange blossoms and a wedding in the spring. You start looking for more than sex out of him, and you're bound to get hurt."

A hollow sensation churned through Greta's stomach, a yawning emptiness that felt like she hadn't eaten for a week. "You really ought to learn to come right out and say what you think, Maxine."

"Hey, I'm sorry, but that's the way I see it. It comes out differently, I'll be your bridesmaid."

Greta's joy of just a few minutes earlier had withered to a dull ache behind her eyes. "I gotta go."

"Honey, don't be mad at me," Maxine said. "I just want you to see life from an objective viewpoint. It doesn't mean you can't have one hell of a good time with Adam, even if he *is* a principal."

Greta flipped absently through the mail she was still holding. "I guess there's a kernel of truth in what you're saying. It's just that Adam might be different. He seems to truly mean what he says."

"Sure," Maxine said. "One good thing, at least we can be certain he's not just after your money."

"Thanks. You're all heart."

The way she felt at the moment, Greta knew she couldn't look at Maxine without bursting into tears. She sat there, sorting through her mail. Maxine had hit a raw nerve. No question about it. Maybe it was best if she didn't go into an affair with all her defenses down. If Adam was interested in only a sexual thing, maybe she could pick up on his intentions, avoid a little heartache. Then again, maybe not.

Greta stacked all the telephone messages into a neat little pile. One by one, she unfolded the homework assignments and ironed out the wrinkles with her hand. A plain white envelope fell to her lap. She reached inside and removed a single sheet of white paper. The words were scrawled in pencil.

"What's the matter?" Maxine asked. "You just turned as white as Cecelia Hartman's ass."

Greta held up the sheet of paper. "This was in my mailbox. It says: 'Mind your own business, or you'll be next.' "

18

GRETA entered the main office searching for Pontrelli. The familiar *click-clack* of Connie's typewriter was missing; not even one reporter hung around looking for a quick interview. The door to Adam's inner office was closed, so she couldn't see through to the conference room beyond. Above her head, a flickering fluorescent light signaled in its maddening way that a replacement bulb was needed. Greta hurried down the hall to the other entrance to the conference room and peeked through the partially open door.

Pontrelli sat alone, flipping through the ragged pages of his little notebook, a ballpoint pen behind his ear. He looked up when he saw Greta, jerking his head in a gesture that seemed to indicate it was okay to enter. She walked in and dropped the threatening note on the table in front of him.

Pontrelli didn't touch the note. He looked at it closely, examined the words. Greta gazed out the window at the heavy gray clouds rolling in from the west. Maybe the first rainstorm of the season was approaching, or maybe there just wasn't enough gloom settled on McCormick High already.

Finally Pontrelli said, "I guess your fingerprints are all over this by now. We'll have to take your prints, then run a check for additional ones."

"Well, I did have to touch it to read it, you know," she said. "My fingerprints are on file with the board of education."

"Amateurs. I'll have one of my people redo them so I'm sure we get a good set."

"So what do you think?"

"One of the hazards in this line of work," he said. "The bad guys don't like it when you get too close."

"You think Rudy Smith found out I went to his dentist's office? I mean, how could he possibly know?"

"I just talked to the head custodian. Seems Smith came in this morning and took some stuff out of his locker, but then the head lost track of him. Guy thought Rudy was making his rounds, sweeping, cleaning the drinking fountains, his usual morning routine. But the fountains were never touched. Same for the sweeping. Rudy probably went into the main office, left the note for the principal, and took off."

"So he had planned to quit before he ever got here," Greta said.

"Sure looks that way. The head custodian said he never punched in on his time card, just grabbed his personal things and left the note." Pontrelli jerked his head toward the note written to Greta. "Maybe he left two notes."

Greta sat down even though she hadn't been invited. "Isn't he acting a little too suspicious? I mean, up until I went to the dental clinic, I was the only one who suspected Rudy was the killer."

Pontrelli pinched his eyebrows together. "Mrs. Gallagher, you certainly have a way with words."

"Oh, I didn't mean it that way . . . I mean, not exactly."

"You meant every word, not that I blame you. Thanks to you, I got Zamora out there right now, getting a formal statement from the dentist."

"Great, then you've got him!"

"Not yet. This won't help Smith, the fact that he contrived an alibi, but it won't hang him, either."

Greta wasn't certain she understood. "What do you mean, it won't hang him?"

"Circumstantial. All we got is circumstantial. I just sent another detective and some uniforms over to his place with a warrant, but I doubt it's going to mean much."

"Well," Greta said, "you may find a clue. You may even find Rudy."

Pontrelli stared at her for a moment. "Not likely. My guess is Smith's on the road somewhere, probably heading out of town as fast as his motorcycle can carry him."

"Well, can't you do something to stop him? I still think the fact that he quit his job is important." Greta crossed her legs and leaned back in her chair. "But, on the other hand, if he is the killer, wouldn't he try to appear innocent? He's practically advertising his guilt by running away."

"Maybe he figures it's too late. You busted his alibi wide open, remember?"

Greta shook her head. "It still doesn't fit. It isn't like Rudy's acting; it's more like he's reacting."

Pontrelli narrowed his puffy eyes into puffy slits. Some of his gruffness had fallen away. Could it be he actually appreciated her sticking her neck out to catch Rudy in his lie? Impossible, yet he *was* treating her differently.

"Mrs. Gallagher, you've lost me." His tone of voice was almost respectful, as if he valued her opinion. Almost.

"Please, call me Greta," she said. Something was wrong with all this, but she couldn't quite put her finger on it. "Let's go back over what Rudy did today."

"Go ahead."

"Well, if he arrived on time, he got here before eight. Probably seven-thirty or so."

"Yeah." Pontrelli answered with a touch of impatience in his voice, but not the usual snap.

She spoke faster. "Okay, so he goes to his locker, takes out his personal possessions, then leaves a letter of resignation in the principal's mailbox."

"Also a little love note for you."

Greta shook her head. "I don't think so. Even Rudy wouldn't be that stupid. Besides, why would he threaten me *before* I went to the clinic? He could have done what he had to do in twenty minutes or less. I never left campus until the beginning of the second class period. I didn't arrive at the clinic until after nine."

Pontrelli nodded. "I see what you're getting at. Not bad, Mrs. . . . uh, Greta."

"That could only mean what you suggested the other day, two different killers. Maybe Rudy had a disagreement with Irene and tried to make it look like Belinda's murderer had done both killings. One of those copycat crimes. Or maybe Rudy and the other killer are in this together somehow."

"Not bad," Pontrelli repeated, "but we still got some holes as big as the captain's ass, pardon my French. I got no motives, nobody placing Smith or anybody else at the scene of either crime, and just about anybody we could name could have had the opportunity. Except for the necktie, we're still talking circumstantial."

"But don't you think the necktie was stolen from Stanley's room on purpose? Someone wanted to make it look like Stanley was involved?"

Pontrelli shrugged. "Yeah, it could've been a frame, or maybe all those ties were just convenient. I also found out Mr. Deep doesn't lock his classroom door when he goes to lunch, so anybody could have grabbed one of his ties."

Greta said, "Then you're certain the necktie was the murder weapon?"

"The girl's blood was all over it. Yeah, that's pretty certain."

"Well, at least you know Stanley is innocent in spite of the necktie. He was in the lunchroom with me and about thirty other teachers when Irene was killed."

Pontrelli rubbed his chin. She could hear the scraping of the stubble of his beard against his rough fingers. Getting close to Pontrelli would probably be a lot like fondling a cactus.

"Yeah, I remember Deep's alibi. Him and just about every other male teacher on the campus had somebody to vouch for him. And the Bench kid was still in Juvie. He was released this morning, by the way."

"Finally," Greta said. "I can't imagine what took you so long."

"Just the usual red tape. Pisses off the public, that's why we drag out the process with all our forms and releases."

Greta smiled. Why had she thought Pontrelli was a lot like Carl? Carl never had a sense of humor, at least not about himself.

"Well," she said, "I'm glad T.P.'s out of there. Don't forget Rudy Smith no longer has an alibi."

Pontrelli looked at her out of the corner of one eye. "I remember."

"Don't you think Rudy must have killed Irene?"

"Let's say the chances are pretty good that Smith is our man, but let's also leave the door open for the chance that we got two, or more, perps involved," Pontrelli said. "That means if we do find Smith, and I'm certain we will, we're still not finished."

Greta said, "Rudy might know who the other person is. Can't you force it out of him when you question him? Lean on him until he talks?"

"Television," Pontrelli said. "Damned box has turned my job into a piece of cake. Everything solved before the last commercial."

137

"That isn't what I meant. I just thought you could some-how . . . Well, I guess I did think you could make him talk like they do on TV."

Carefully touching only one corner, he picked up the note Greta had brought to him. "Sure, Smith might spill his guts, if he knows anything. It ain't always as easy as the scriptwriters want you to believe." He pulled a crumpled plastic bag from his jacket pocket and wriggled the note inside. "I gotta get this thing dusted for prints and then see if the handwriting pros want to take a look at it. Looks to me like a right-hander printed it with his left hand."

Greta stood up and smoothed the wrinkles out of the front of her skirt. "I didn't mean to take up so much of your time, I just wanted you to see this note."

"You did the right thing," Pontrelli said. "We also have to talk about some police protection for you."

"Whatever for?" Greta said with an embarrassed laugh. "This could be from anyone, even from a student who finds this sort of thing amusing."

Pontrelli looked at Greta, lines carved deep into his leathery face. "Well, I ain't amused one least bit, and until we get somewhere with this case, now I gotta worry about the killer getting his hands around your neck."

19

"WHAT do you mean, you refused police protection?" Adam said. The veins in his neck stuck out like thick white cords against his reddened skin. "That's crazy. It may take them days to catch Smith."

Greta continued chopping thin slices from a mound of fresh mushrooms on the cutting board. "How could I spend the night here with you if I had a cop tailing me?"

Beyond the two large picture windows on the north wall of Adam's kitchen lay total darkness, with the bright room mirrored in the black reflection. Outside, the threat of rain was still just a threat, but thick clouds had blotted out the moon and stars.

No chance for even a romantic walk in the moonlight, but still she had elevated her first night at Adam's house into some kind of Cinderella–Prince Charming thing. She needed to work on this fantasy affliction of hers. They were cooking dinner together. Period. Yet, she had pumped it up into a Hollywood production. Maybe she should check her shoes. She just might be prancing about Adam's kitchen in glass slippers.

No, she hadn't wanted to postpone this night with Adam, and she certainly didn't want to do it with the LAPD looking over her shoulder. She especially didn't want Pontrelli to know she was romantically involved with Adam. It was crazy for her to think Pontrelli accepted her on a "professional" level, yet for some reason she couldn't explain, she wanted to maintain Pontrelli's respect.

Adam said, "What difference does it make if a couple of cops figure out we're lovers? They're not going to run to the superintendent with the news. Besides, we don't need to keep it to ourselves, except at school. It's not like either of us is married."

Greta sprinkled the sliced mushrooms over the lettuce she had torn into mouth-size pieces. "This morning you said we had to be circumspect. Having a police car sit in your driveway all night is not circumspect. Besides, I just wouldn't feel comfortable."

Adam turned on the indoor electric grill and adjusted the thermostat. He owned every conceivable kitchen appliance, from a digital coffee brewer to a trash compactor, including several that Greta couldn't even identify. A cupboard, bigger than Greta's refrigerator, housed a pasta maker, an espresso machine, the latest Cuisinart food processor, and half a dozen shiny, impressive gadgets that must be known only to the wealthy. Cooking with all this stuff had probably been second nature to Adam's wife. Hadn't he said she used to cook gourmet meals? Greta passed on the gadgetry and did her slicing and chopping by hand.

Adam sat down next to the work center where Greta was now rinsing a handful of green beans. He stretched both arms above his shoulders and gyrated his head into a couple of neck rolls. "You're not helping the tension in my neck, you know? The police are there to help us."

"I know."

"I guess in my position I should be grateful you want to be discreet, but the thought of that maniac threatening you makes my blood boil."

Greta dried her hands and went to him. She ran her fingers

through his thick hair, leaned over, kissed him lightly on the forehead. "Stop worrying. No one is going to get anywhere near me—except you, of course."

Adam smiled. "Sounds like the best idea so far. Hey, don't you want to use the automatic steamer?"

Greta had just pulled a steamer pot from the cupboard under the stove. The lid was dusty—she should have guessed that a space-age replacement for the old standby lurked around here somewhere.

"No, I'm not into all your high-tech contraptions. My cooking is pretty simple, and I'm used to old-fashioned pots and pans, the kind that Mother used to throw at dear old Dad."

"Did she really?"

"No, I made that part up, but I'm still cooking with pots my mother bought over thirty years ago, and they seem to work just fine."

"Suit yourself, but once you get used to my gadgets, you'll never want to be without." He gave her a playful peck on the cheek, then reached over and pressed the TV remote control, bringing a color picture into focus on the white-rimmed set that was imbedded into the wall near the breakfast nook. This kitchen lacked nothing.

"Hey," Greta said, "I thought we weren't going to watch any more news tonight?"

"Just a quick look. I want to see if they found Smith."

Adam had activated Fox News. The reporter was discussing the aborted takeoff of a DC-10 at Los Angeles International Airport. Passengers were shaken, but no one was injured.

"Next," the reporter said, "an update on the two brutal slayings at McCormick High in the San Fernando Valley."

Greta dropped the beans into the steamer rack and turned to watch the report. The hair on her forearms rose. The smiling senior portraits of both Belinda and Irene, taken just weeks ago, covered the screen.

The reporter went on. "As police continue their search for Rudy Smith, a school custodian who is wanted for questioning, Adam Mason, the embattled principal of McCormick High, reports that attendance was off almost seventy percent today. According to Mason, students and parents are scared. Kids just don't want to go to school. A school employee disclosed that she has received applications for twenty-eight permits for transfers to another school."

"That's Vera," Greta said when the camera moved in closer. "Did you know about this?"

Adam shook his head and stared at the screen while Vera explained that some permits came with transportation, meaning school busing, others did not.

The reporter in the field, a young woman, pressed closer to Vera. "Wouldn't this mean that a student might have to travel a great distance, at his or her own expense, even if a permit is granted?"

Vera straightened her shoulders and wiggled her nose just slightly. The district superintendent couldn't have looked or sounded more official. "Well, first the permit has to be approved by the receiving school, but yes, the students would have to travel out of their regular school area at their own expense. Of course, that might be less of a problem than what we've got here. You can't run a normal school day if the kids are too scared to go to classes."

Greta slapped at the controls, blacking out Vera and her words. She wanted this whole thing to be over. She wanted the case solved, so their lives at McCormick could return to normal. Two murders on campus. A threatening note obviously from someone other than Rudy, someone the police weren't even searching for since they didn't have so much as a clue in Belinda's case. She couldn't even fully enjoy her new romance while her mind throbbed with visions of Belinda lying dead in the workroom and Irene being murdered in a parking lot.

Adam gently massaged his closed eyelids with his fingertips, positioning his hand so that it covered his face even after he stopped rubbing.

Greta said, "Vera should have more sense, running on like that. Aren't the kids scared enough?"

Adam nodded. "That interview was one I missed. I thought I had seen all the news reports they filmed today. Lord knows I witnessed at least five or six, plus all the times they interviewed me personally."

Greta adjusted the flame under the steamer. "Damned reporters are oozing out of the woodwork. I had to duck into the ladies' room to avoid one before I left today."

"Then the press doesn't know about the note, that you were threatened?"

"No, and I for one don't plan to tell them. They'll be all over me once they find out."

Adam stood up and began to pace. Greta had never noticed before now that Adam resorted to this agitated form of pacing. He reeled back and forth in a very short space, circling almost enough to make her dizzy. Maybe it was something he did only under severe stress, like when his world was crumbling faster than he could say "pasta machine."

He finally stopped moving and said, "You may be right. I think you should keep the note you received quiet, but I still think you should take whatever police protection Pontrelli can offer."

"I'll think about it, okay? But I didn't want to spoil tonight. I can always talk to Pontrelli tomorrow."

Adam walked over to her and placed his hands around her waist. "Don't be a hero, all right?"

"Definitely. When will you be ready to put the salmon on the grill?"

"I'm ready now. Just say the word." He removed a plate holding two bright pink fillets from the refrigerator. He stood there for a moment, a frown puckering his face. "Greta, do you see me as embattled?"

She thought for a moment. "Well, I hadn't thought of you exactly as 'embattled.' I guess it's a favorite catchword of the fourth estate, but it doesn't really mean anything. Why, does it bother you?"

"It's just that if the press says it often enough, the parents of our students, and then the school board, will also see me in that light."

Greta took the plate from his hand and set it on the counter. "Listen, if they transfer you to Timbuktu, maybe I could get a transfer, too. We could carpool."

Adam took her in his arms. "I would never let you sacrifice your career for me. I know how hard you've worked. Don't worry, somehow this will all work out."

Greta smiled. If she could be this happy a few hours after receiving a threatening note from a murderer, how could anything ruin what they had going? Maxine was wrong about Adam. She had to be. Adam was everything Carl had never been. Adam wasn't riddled with faults like Carl; he was perfect. But then, that wasn't possible, was it? No one is perfect. Hadn't her mother drummed that little aphorism into her head years ago?

But Maxine was certainly wrong about Adam's relationship with Greta. It wasn't strictly physical, even though Greta was looking forward to the view from Adam's upstairs bedroom tonight. What they had was special, a meeting of two minds with a little lust thrown in to make it more exciting.

"Well," she said, "let's get to work. You do want to eat dinner before midnight, don't you?"

Adam picked up a long loaf of French bread from the counter and held it football style. He faked a pass, then tossed it at her over his shoulder. "If you insist, but right now I'm more interested in postdinner activities."

144

She caught the bread before it hit the floor. Greta was right about Adam. She had to be. She felt too happy for it not to be right, and she was determined that not even a murdering madman would spoil her joy.

20

WEDNESDAY night, the storm finally moved in and clobbered the Los Angeles basin. Early the next morning Adam switched on the weather forecast in the master bathroom while he shaved.

Greta pulled herself up to one elbow as soon as she heard the radio. Her neck felt funny; a little ache twinged across her shoulder blades. Must be from the strange pillow. Her one eye was glued shut, but she spotted the time, glowing in green from a digital clock next to the bed. She fumbled with her flimsy negligee, wishing she had her comfortable old terry cloth robe instead.

The announcer's voice was loud and resonant, but Greta picked up only pieces of the report. "The low pressure system should linger at least two days . . . The first measurable rain to fall in Los Angeles since last June . . . Allow plenty of extra time for your commute to work . . . Flooding reported at some intersections already . . . Expect the rain to be very heavy at times." He went on and on. Rain was always big news in Los Angeles.

Greta listened to the radio from the bedroom, not wanting to barge in on Adam even though she could see him shaving through the partially open door. She wasn't ready to share a bathroom with him just yet, and she wasn't up to seeking out another one on the second floor even though she was certain a house this size had a bath connected to each bedroom. She found her overnight bag and put on her underwear, brand new, while she waited for Adam to finish.

Damn, she wished she'd brought along a pair of pants instead of her burgundy wool suit. All the working women in Los Angeles wore pants on days like this, or else they wore long skirts and high boots, gaucho style. She always wore pants, old pants, when it rained, but ever since Adam had made the comment about her shapely ankles, she had worn nothing but skirts. After all, Adam couldn't admire her ankles if they were covered with a pair of pants, now could he?

Of course her thinking was stupid, but since she felt she had so few good points in the looks department, flaunting whatever Adam found appealing couldn't hurt. At least she had brought along a warm turtleneck sweater to wear with her suit. While she was packing for the evening, she had also come across an old white blouse with a fussy lace collar. God, it was a Cecelia-style thing she hadn't even known she owned. She'd immediately stuffed the blouse into a bag of clothing she was saving for the Salvation Army. Was it possible Greta herself had been headed for a life as a crotchety old biddy without even realizing it?

They hurried through breakfast and decided it would be sensible to take just one car out into the storm. Greta didn't protest leaving her car safely inside Adam's garage. After all, this meant she would have to return later in the day, or perhaps tonight.

The rain pummeled the windshield of Adam's car in big, explosive drops. No rain at all for months and then a downpour that would transform some of the city streets into rivers. The gray sky, mottled with thick, black clouds, looked like the wrong backdrop for the towering palm trees that now leaned away from the gusting wind. It was very easy to let yourself get spoiled by the usually sunny weather in Los Angeles.

Adam inched the car down the winding hills of Laurel Canyon, his headlights reflecting off the wet sheen of the many layers of built-up oil on the road's surface. Greta tried to think of something to say, something clever, or even just cheerful, but her mind flickered on another level, playing reruns of last night. She wanted this feeling to last for about a hundred years.

The windshield wipers sloshed back and forth, battling unsuccessfully with the torrents of rain. An oncoming car raced through a flooded intersection, drenching Adam's car windows with a sudden burst of water. Greta jumped even though the interior of the car remained perfectly dry.

"Look at that nut," Adam said, gripping the wheel so tightly his knuckles showed white. "People just don't understand how dangerous it is to speed through intersections when the streets are flooded like this."

"I know," Greta agreed, not really caring.

Carl had also griped about other drivers, cursing and flipping them off if the offense was great enough, and she used to hate it. Carl had always made such a fuss, acting like he had some God-given right to the road. Funny, with Adam it didn't bother her. Did she see it as a natural extension of his position? After all, Adam was an authority figure in a large urban high school. Principals and teachers were supposed to correct erring students, weren't they? God, was this a case of overrationalization, or what?

Adam waited in line at the on ramp to the Hollywood Freeway north. In spite of the many drivers speeding mindlessly over the wet canyon roads, once they hit the busier streets, traffic crept along at an agonizing pace. Ahead, the less-traveled northern lanes of the freeway were snarled, the pavement glowing red with reflections of brake lights. The southbound lanes weren't moving at all; probably the first of many accidents for the day had already happened.

Days like this were meant for lazing in front of a fire with a good book, not for heading off to work in a school filled with cops, security people, TV reporters, and plenty of fear.

"If we had seventy percent absent yesterday," Greta said, "I guess we won't have any kids at all today."

Adam nodded without taking his eyes off the road. "We may have to improvise. I was thinking of having all the kids who do show up report to the library, along with a skeleton crew of counselors. Maybe I'll run a few short staff meetings during the day, brief the teachers on what's happening. I've heard some complaints that I'm not keeping the teachers posted on the case. Trouble is, we have so little to report."

"I haven't heard any complaints about you from Maxine," Greta said. "But then, I guess I've been too busy to talk much with Max."

"Strikes me as strange that the two of you are so close. She's so different from you."

Greta smiled to herself. "I know Max comes on like some wild-eyed Carrie Nation, swinging a big ax, but she really has a heart of gold. I wouldn't have made it through the last three years without her."

"That's how long you've been divorced?" he asked.

"Yes, but I'm not just talking about her moral support during my divorce. She literally dragged me to union meetings and encouraged me to get involved with school-based management. I wouldn't be working on the management team now if it weren't for Max."

"Then I'm glad you're buddies. As I see it, school-based management is the only thing that will pull us out of the mess we've gotten ourselves into."

"I didn't think most principals liked us stepping on their toes."

Adam chuckled. "I'm no fool. I can see it's going to take more than one person to solve our problems."

"Then you agree we need to reform the way L.A. schools are run?"

"Damn straight. I look forward to the input of you and the others on the team. The work you're doing makes a lot of sense."

"So how come you never said that at any of our meetings?"

"I guess I needed you to inspire me. Maybe I'll say it at the next meeting, okay?"

When Adam finally pulled into the principal's parking space, the cold reality of the school sitting there, sheeted in rain, reminded her that a killer or two still roamed about. School-based management couldn't save McCormick from the stigma of this kind of reputation.

"I'd better check in with Vera and the other counselors," she said.

"Okay, my sweet." Adam looked around, apparently checking to see if they had an audience. He squeezed her knee, but stopped short of a kiss. "I'll see you later."

Greta tried to wrest open her folding umbrella for the short dash from the car to the overhang protecting the main gate, but the wind fought back. She gave up on the umbrella and made a run for it while Adam locked the car and retrieved his briefcase from the trunk. Driven sideways by the wind, the rain lashed against her legs, plastering her pantyhose against those visibly shapely ankles. What a moron she was, worse than the high school girls who wouldn't wear a jacket on cold days because jackets weren't "in." Tomorrow she would wear pants.

The early morning light shone dimly through the windows of the counseling office. Vera sat at her desk, which was not in a private cubicle but right in the center of the room. The battered old desk abutted a similar one used by a part-time file clerk. Vera clattered away on an ancient IBM Selectric typewriter, grunting but not even looking up when Greta called hello. No sense starting up with Vera. Once Vera got going, Greta wouldn't be able to turn her off.

The campus was far too quiet. Greta listened for the familiar giggling and deep-throated laughter that always accompanied groups of teenagers. Nothing. Only the clacking of Vera's typewriter and the steady drip of the rain. She went inside her office but didn't close the door. There was something comforting about the sound of Vera's industrious presence.

Unanswered notes, phone messages, and everything that had been in her mailbox yesterday, except for the threatening note, lay in a haphazard scatter across her desk. She sat down and stared at the mess as if the paperwork itself might tell her where to begin. A slight shuffling noise at her office door broke her concentration.

"T.P.!" Greta shouted as soon as she saw who it was.

She jumped up and ushered the boy to a chair. Dark patches of purple ringed both his eyes, eyes that had apparently seen more in a few short days than most kids witness in all their teenage years.

"I'm so glad you stopped in," Greta said. "How're you doing?"

"Well, now that I'm out of Juvie, I feel better, I guess. I just don't understand what's going on around here. They told me about Irene."

Greta nodded. "We've got a sick person out there somewhere. A very sick person."

"Detective Pontrelli told me you went to bat for me right from the beginning. Said you kept insisting they were wrong, that I didn't do it."

"Pontrelli said that?"

T.P. rubbed the back of his hand across his mouth. "Yeah, he said you just wouldn't let up. You were about to drive him nuts."

Greta wanted to laugh and cry at the same time. "I guess Pontrelli would put it in those words," she said mostly to herself.

"There's going to be a memorial service for Belinda and Irene on Monday. Juan's mother told me."

"You talked to Juan?"

T.P. looked down and shook his head. "No, he couldn't talk. His mother said he was under sedation."

Greta reached over and patted his hand. "T.P., I know the police have asked you a thousand questions, but I wondered if there was anything, anything at all, you may have remembered that you haven't told them."

"I think I told them everything, I just know I didn't kill Belinda. I could never kill Belinda."

"Of course you couldn't," Greta said, "but I'm curious about what she said when she broke up with you. You do know you were not the father of her baby?"

T.P.'s ears and throat turned scarlet. He looked as if he were about to cry. "Yeah, they told me."

"Did she give you any idea who the other guy might have been? Did you ever see her talking to anyone? Did she mention any other guys as being . . . well, good friends?"

He shook his head. "She never mentioned any names, but I had a lot of time to think while they had me locked up, and I remembered something."

"What, T.P.? What did you remember?"

"Whoever the guy was, he must have been older than me. A lot older."

T.P.'s words stuck her like a fishhook. "What makes you say that?"

T.P. hesitated. When he finally spoke, he spoke to the floor. "The last month or so, maybe even longer, Belinda kept saying things about me being immature. One time she said all high

152

school boys must be socially retarded, and she didn't think I'd ever catch up with her."

"Did she say she liked older guys better?"

T.P. shook his head. "Not exactly in those words, but she started talking about 'men' as if she knew the difference between going out with a guy like me and someone a lot older. I didn't believe she actually had someone else, but then the cops told me about the baby."

"T.P., this could be important. If she had a relationship going with an older man, he could also be the one who killed her."

He blinked back tears, and Greta immediately regretted having said that. The poor kid had been tortured enough without her beating home her point, but after a few moments he swallowed hard and recovered somewhat.

T.P. said, "I thought and thought about the way she criticized me for always thinking and acting like a kid. Things I've always done, like horsing around with Juan or one of the other guys, really set her off. She said Juan and me were totally immature, so I guess that's it. She was running around behind my back with some older guy."

"T.P., this is important. Do you have any idea who it could have been?"

"I dunno. I guess she was pretty careful about not getting caught when she cheated on me."

T.P. looked like he had never said anything more painful. She hated the agony in his voice and the defeat in his eyes.

Greta spoke slowly, almost tasting the words. "Listen, maybe it wasn't as bad as you think. Maybe Belinda didn't go out looking for another man, but maybe this someone approached her, gave her enough sweet talk to sweep her off her feet. Sometimes these things happen very fast." She didn't know how long it had taken Belinda to fall for her older man. Greta's own capitulation to Adam was probably something for the Guinness Book of World Records.

T.P. said, "But who?"

"Have you heard the police are looking for one of our custodians, Rudy Smith?"

"Yeah, I heard that. Do they figure he had something to do with Irene's murder?"

"Possibly," Greta said. "But don't you see, Rudy could have something to do with Belinda as well. Rudy could have been the older man in Belinda's life."

T.P. shook his head violently. "Nah, no way. I don't know who it was, but I know it wasn't Rudy Smith."

Greta watched T.P. carefully. His eyes had suddenly gone blank, and she couldn't read the same emotions he had registered only moments ago. "But how do you know it wasn't Rudy?"

"Easy," T.P. said. "She hated Rudy. He fixed her locker for her once, and he tried to hit on her. She said he was dirty, he had bad breath, and she hated being anywhere near him. She told me she'd rather carry her books around all day long, no matter how heavy they were, than risk having him fix her locker again."

"Did Belinda tell anyone else, any of her teachers, that Rudy came on to her?"

T.P. squeezed his fingers around the arm of the chair. "I told her to tell you or one of her teachers about Rudy. Scum like him shouldn't be allowed to work at a school. Do they know for sure that he killed Irene?"

"So far they just want to question him," Greta hedged, "but let's get back to my question. Belinda didn't tell me Rudy came on to her. Did she report it to one of her teachers?"

"Sure, but it wasn't a teacher. She went directly to the principal. She told Mr. Mason."

21

GRETA talked to T.P. for a few more minutes, but his words coalesced into meaningless noise, lost in the echoes shivering through her mind. Belinda had gone to Adam with her problem, told him about Rudy's advance. Adam had never mentioned this to her. Had he told the police?

A few minutes later, T.P. explained he had to go. Greta got up and hugged him, a move that seemed to please and embarrass T.P. at the same time. Greta walked down the hall to the main office. She had to talk to Adam. He couldn't have forgotten Belinda's reporting that Rudy had been offensive, no matter how veiled Rudy's advance might have been, not in light of her murder right here on campus.

The door to Adam's private office was closed, not slightly ajar the way he usually left it if he were just chatting with a teacher or student, but shut tight. Greta spotted Adam's secretary, Connie, grappling with a decrepit ditto machine off in the corner of the main office. Connie mumbled to herself as she tried to fasten a splotchy blue-and-white master to the drum of the machine.

"Connie, is Adam in his office?" Greta asked.

Connie looked up and smiled. A purplish blue smudge of duplicating fluid glistened on the tip of her nose. "Yeah, with

Detective Pontrelli and that other one, the woman. They didn't look too happy when they went in there."

"Okay, I guess I can wait. Tell him I'll be in Maxine Kramer's room if he should ask."

Greta gathered two lone messages from her mailbox. Definitely not a normal school day if this was all her mailbox held. Stanley Deep walked over to her. His pale green polyester slacks and striped golf shirt almost matched, and she could even forgive his after-shave. Under his arm, he carried a clear plastic raincoat folded up into a flattened wad. At least he wasn't wearing one of his hideous neckties.

"Did you see the detectives go into the boss's office?" he asked.

"No, what's up?"

Stanley raised both hands, palms up, indicating he was not on top of the gossip for a change. "I heard them ask for Mason, then they all went inside and closed the door. God, I hope they haven't found another girl."

"Don't even think that, Stanley. I don't think I can take any more of this maniac, whoever he is."

Stanley looked at her out of the corner of his eye. "Are you being coy with me?"

"What do you mean?"

"I've heard, everybody's heard, that you suspected Rudy from the very beginning. Long before the police started looking for him."

Damn that Vera. She sure hadn't wasted any time spreading the news.

Greta said, "Well, Stanley, you heard right. What else might the grapevine be spewing out these days?"

"Hey, don't be mad at me. I think it's great how you picked up on that little slime bag before the cops did. Shows you have a line on what's going on around here. The cops sure as hell don't know what's happening."

Greta didn't answer. She pushed open the door to the outside, shivering slightly from the rush of brisk air and the thick gloom of the rain. As gray and dreary as it was, at least the air smelled fresh. She breathed deeply, hoping the rain-cleansed air was therapeutic.

Stanley unfolded his plastic raincoat and slipped it on. He trotted outside after her. "Hey, where are you going? You walked right by the counseling office."

"I know. I thought I'd go talk to Maxine for a while. There can't be more than ten students on campus. Vera can handle the crush for a few minutes."

Stanley held the door for her. "Well, if you're going all the way over to the art rooms, you'd better let me walk with you."

Greta looked at him. He was serious. "Why, Stanley?"

Stanley avoided Greta's eyes and, instead, concentrated intently on buttoning his raincoat, like a kid who had just learned how to dress himself. "No need for you to walk by yourself. The way things are, I'll feel better if you're not alone."

"Thanks, Stanley, that's very sweet of you."

Stanley smiled, and Greta visualized a puppy who had just been praised and patted for being a good dog.

"Seems like such a waste," Stanley said, "paying all of us to be here when there are no classes to teach. I've even gotten caught up on most of my committee work."

"You sure spend a lot of time serving on committees. Maxine says we shouldn't be so eager to volunteer. Actually, you're doing administrative work for no extra pay."

Stanley said, "I know I'm a patsy, but I don't mind. It gives me something to do after school. Don't you serve on that management thing?"

"That's different. We get paid for our time. It's in the contract."

"Oh," Stanley said. "Well, the Textbook Committee and

the Scholarship Committee are worthwhile. I don't mind spending my time."

Greta looked at him, trying to figure out why any teacher could possibly need extra activities to keep busy. "Well, unless they pay us for committee work, I plan to turn down all offers. You could spend your time on your lesson plans."

"I've done all my planning for the rest of the semester. Have everything blocked out by the week—that is, if we ever have a next week."

"Yeah, but think of the stories you'll be able to tell by the fire someday, the days of murder at McCormick High."

Stanley stopped walking and shot her a look of surprise. "You're the last one I expected to take these murders lightly. Are you feeling all right?"

"I'm sorry. I don't know what made me say that. Believe me, I don't take any of this lightly."

"Watch that puddle." Stanley took her arm and led her around a section of the walkway that was not draining onto the already saturated grass. A battalion of snails had sought the higher ground of the concrete, depositing their slick trails upon the wet pavement. Drowned earthworms ringed the edges of the puddles.

"Thanks," Greta said, stepping around the snails and the bloated worms.

"You know what I think?" Stanley said. "I think they had no right to stick you in the middle of this mess the way they did. The cops could have found some way of interrogating the kids without making you sit in. You're probably under far too much stress."

"Maybe. I don't know. But it wasn't Pontrelli's idea for me to sit in on the interviews. It was Adam's."

Stanley grunted. "Well, Adam should have more sense, and he should do the interviews himself, so you don't have to be involved with something this gruesome."

"Well, perhaps the worst is over," Greta said.

"I hope so. You should be more careful. This kind of pressure isn't good for your health."

"Why, thank you, Stanl—"

"In fact, why don't we go to the happy hour at El Presidente this afternoon? A couple of margaritas will help you unwind from all of this, do you good."

Greta almost laughed out loud. Just when she was about to welcome Stanley to the human race, he reverted back to good ol' Stanley the Lech. "I don't think so," she said. "But maybe some other time."

"Sure," he said, again not meeting her eyes. "I stop in for a drink almost every day. It's better than going home stone sober."

Greta suddenly realized where poor misunderstood Stanley was coming from. "Is it that bad at home?"

"Some days it's bad, some days it's worse. If it weren't for the kids, I would've left years ago. I live with Barbara, but sometimes I get so lonely just for someone to talk to . . ." Stanley sounded tired. "Well, I didn't mean to trouble you with my problems."

The doors to Maxine's room were wide open in spite of the rain. Greta faced Stanley. "You know, when things return to normal around here, we're going to go have those margaritas. I'll talk Maxine into coming along and the three of us will have a blast."

Stanley grinned. "Great."

"We might even find some other willing souls and turn it into a real party."

"Okay, Greta, I'm gonna hold you to this," Stanley said, still smiling.

Stanley turned and walked away. His excitement had been childlike, and over nothing more than a colleague's agreeing to have a drink with him.

Maxine came to the door and stood with her hands on her hips. Her earrings bobbed back and forth with each exaggerated gesture of her head. "What're you doing out there? Why don't you come inside?"

Greta walked into the room.

Maxine reached into her pocket for a pack of gum. She held out a stick for Greta. "Was that Stanley you were talking to?"

"Yeah. You know, I think we've been too hard on him, knocking him the way we do. He's really a sad case, pathetic actually."

"Pathetic is not one of the qualities I usually look for in a man."

"Okay, but maybe we've been thinking of Stanley in terms of an 'available' man, which, of course, he isn't. We should think of him as a person, a human being. He's really lonely; he needs a couple of friends."

Maxine's eyes narrowed. "Why do I get the feeling that you've just volunteered me to be one of his buddies?"

Greta shook her head. Maxine was the only friend Greta had ever had who could zero in on her thoughts like that. Sometimes it was frightening. "Listen, Max, how much could it hurt us to go out for a drink with Stanley? Maybe we could get a couple of other teachers to go along and turn it into an after-school party. Stanley needs our help."

"Is this one of those things my mother used to talk about that would do my soul a world of good, like donating my entire allowance to the United Jewish Appeal?"

"Something like that." Greta smiled. "C'mon, let's do it. Maybe we'll be surprised—Stanley might be a lot of fun when we get to know him better."

"Yeah, sure. I'll bet he has a whoopee cushion in the back-seat of his car."

The warning bell sounded. Ten minutes until eight and not a student in sight. Maxine poured tempera paint from a large, clumsy plastic jar into small, individual-size containers. "Look at this. Even my T.A.'s don't show up."

Greta said, "Max, can I bounce something off you?"

Maxine finished pouring the paint and screwed the cap back on the jar. She wiped her hands down the front of her jeans. "So what's the matter? Second thoughts about Adam, or did he make you submit a written evaluation of his sexual performance for the school newspaper?"

"You wish. That way you could read all about it, couldn't you?" Greta walked over to one of the open doors. "Mind if I close the doors for a little while?"

"No, go ahead. I'll get the other one."

When both doors were closed, Maxine sat on top of the table closest to Greta. She pulled her knees up to her chin and locked her arms around her legs. "I'm all ears."

Greta hesitated. "I just talked to T.P."

"No kidding? Is he all right?"

"He looks kind of tired and maybe even a bit older, as if he grew up overnight."

"A visit to Juvenile Hall can do that to you."

Greta went on. "T.P. believes Belinda was having an affair with an older man."

"No shit. Well, that makes sense with her being pregnant and then being murdered."

"T.P. also said something that bothered me, about Belinda and Rudy Smith."

"What?"

"Well, it seems Rudy came on to Belinda, and T.P. told her to report it. Instead of telling me or one of her teachers, she told Adam."

"Adam never mentioned this to you?" Maxine asked.

"Never."

"Maybe Belinda was exaggerating Rudy's intentions?"

"Maybe."

Maxine leaned forward, moving into a cross-legged position. "Grets, what's the bottom line here? What do you think it means?"

"I wish I knew. Adam could have dismissed it as unimportant; it happened a week or two before her death. Or perhaps . . ."

"Perhaps he knows something about Rudy Smith that we don't know, and he's not telling."

Greta's right eyelid twitched. She drew her suit jacket tighter across her chest and held it there even though the room was warm enough. "I can't believe Adam had anything to do with Rudy's exploits. Remember, Rudy is still the chief suspect in Irene's murder."

"Why don't you ask Adam?" Maxine said. Her voice was gentler than usual.

"I will. I just wanted to think about it out loud, with you."

"Grets, my friend, there's one other thing you should think about."

"What?"

"You told me it was possible two different killers murdered Belinda and Irene."

"Definitely a possibility."

Maxine jumped down from the table and sat on the chair next to Greta. "Let me run this by you. Suppose an adult on campus was having an affair with Belinda. Suppose this same adult got her pregnant and didn't want Belinda showing off his baby at PTA meetings. So he kills her to solve the problem."

"Yeah, I figured the same thing, but Irene's death doesn't fit. Irene was killed only five days later. That's not coincidental, and not necessarily the whim of a copycat. We don't have a motive for Irene's murder."

"That one's easy. To shut her up. If Irene knew who Belinda was doing sack time with, she could expose him as the killer."

Greta shook her head. "I also thought of that scenario,

but Irene and Wendy came to me right after Belinda's murder. Irene didn't seem to be harboring any secrets. I really think if Irene knew something about Belinda's death, she would have told me or the police immediately."

"So where does that leave you? One of the respectable pillars of our school community hiring Rudy Smith as a paid assassin?"

"No," Greta said, "I don't buy that either. I think it's more like Rudy Smith somehow witnessed Belinda's murder and then decided to blackmail the killer."

"That doesn't explain Irene's murder."

Greta sighed. "I know. That's what I've been trying to figure out. As Pontrelli would say, we've got a hole as big as the captain's ass."

"You don't think this adult had a thing going with *both* girls, do you?"

"I don't know. At the moment I'm more concerned about Adam's oversight, his not telling anyone that Belinda reported Rudy."

Maxine looked at Greta with unconcealed astonishment. "Grets, you don't think *Adam* was the one having an affair with Belinda, do you?"

Greta's chest tightened against her pounding heart. She could feel Maxine's stare boring into her.

"Of course not! That's the most ridiculous thing I've ever heard."

22

GRETA left Maxine's classroom and headed back toward the administration building. For the past few days the deathly quiet on campus had been unnerving, but now the steady dripping of the rain was enough to drive her mad. Water drummed against the narrow overhang that protected the walkway, and the cold, wet wind blew her already damp hair into her eyes. She pushed it away, while hot, salty tears slid down her cheeks.

What was the matter with her anyway? How could she even think Adam might have had something to do with the murders? How could anyone as warm and loving as Adam nonchalantly strangle the life out of two young girls? It didn't make sense, yet the thoughts had entered her mind just as surely as they had flashed into Maxine's. Adam involved with one or both of the girls? It was ridiculous, wasn't it?

Perhaps, if she were to face the truth, Adam's suddenly falling in love with her was the only ridiculous piece to this whole puzzle. Granted, she wasn't exactly ugly, but she was no raving beauty either. Sure, she had her good features, like her blue eyes and clear skin, and hadn't Adam done a whole god-damn number on her ankles? She couldn't think straight; her thoughts kept returning to the overwhelming fear that she had been used by the man she loved.

Adam, if he indeed did have something to hide, had sensed a need to throw Greta, the bloodhound, off his scent. She had been too eager to defend T.P., too willing to offer her opinions to Pontrelli. By keeping her busy beneath the sheets, he had kept her inquiring mind occupied, at least part of the time. Had her eagerness to believe that Adam loved her blown away all her common sense? Adam must be thrilled his little scam had turned out so well. Dammit, how could she have been so stupid?

She ran into the women's rest room. Puffy, red blotches ringed her eyes. Even when she cried for just a minute or two, she took on the appearance of someone who'd just come off a three-week bender. The pathetic image reflected in the mirror made her doubly certain Adam couldn't possibly be in love with her.

She thought she was going to vomit. She rushed into one of the stalls. Her heart thudding in her ears, she closed her eyes and leaned over the toilet. Her gut wrenched painfully, but nothing came up. Her eyes flickered open. The toilet bowl had a brown ring around the water line and crusted scum wedged under the rim. A foul odor registered, and her hand flew to her mouth to avert the wave of nausea. She had to get out of there.

Greta stopped at the sink and splashed cold water on her face. She did her best to rearrange her hair without a comb, then walked outside. Across the hall, she saw Detective Zamora in the doorway to the main office. As usual, Zamora was scribbling something in her notebook.

Zamora looked up, spotted Greta, then strutted toward her like the tough cops do on TV. Her eyes were cold. She was ready to grill public enemy number one. "We've been looking for you."

"Oh," Greta said, kicking herself because something a bit more intelligent hadn't popped into her mind.

The iciness in Zamora's voice hadn't come close to the

animosity in her eyes. She stared at Greta, one hand defensively fixed on her hip. "You out investigating another crime, or are you still working my turf?"

Greta's knees felt rubbery, but she looked Zamora in the eyes. "Listen, I had no idea you were the one who talked to the receptionist at the dental clinic. I hope I didn't make any trouble for you."

Zamora snickered, sending a slight spray of spit toward Greta's chin, but Greta didn't move to wipe it away.

"Lady, you gotta be kidding."

Greta backed away a few inches, but she maintained eye contact. "No, I mean that. I had this feeling about Rudy Smith from the very beginning. It would be just like him to set himself up with an alibi, but there's no way you could have known that. I had the advantage of seeing him sneak around this campus, leering at people, especially the girls, for the last few years."

"So, if you had this 'feeling' about the guy, why didn't you tell me or Pontrelli instead of taking matters into your own hands?"

Greta said, "But I did tell Detective Pontrelli, the very first day he was on campus. He made me feel like I was a lost little girl who needed to be led home by the wrist. He didn't think I knew what I was talking about."

The sneer on Zamora's face softened. She blinked. "You mean you told Pontrelli about your suspicions after the *first* murder?"

Greta nodded. "Yes, and he made me so mad I wanted to scream."

Zamora frantically thumbed through the first few pages of her notebook. "I don't remember him telling me you reported anything about Smith."

"Well, I told him, for all the good it did. If he had done something about Rudy then, Irene might still be alive."

"Hard to say," Zamora said. She closed the notebook. "Listen, Pontrelli's in the office with the principal. He wants to talk to you."

"What about?"

Zamora shrugged. "Maybe I'd better let him tell you. I don't need to get my head chewed off again."

Greta could imagine what Detective Zamora had to go through when Pontrelli was on a rampage. Greta had thought Zamora was indifferent, unreachable, but perhaps her robotlike manner was her only means of self-defense. Greta followed Zamora to Adam's office. Zamora knocked, and Pontrelli bellowed for them to come in.

Adam sat at his desk. He looked a lot paler than he had when Greta left him an hour or so earlier, but his eyes brightened when he saw her. A large claw ripped at her heart. She had to be paranoid. Adam hadn't used her. He couldn't have.

Pontrelli stood in one corner, leaning against the file cabinet.

Adam said, "I've been trying to find you for the last twenty minutes."

Greta looked at Pontrelli. His face told her nothing, but cryptic vibes emanated from him as surely as if he were a lighthouse beacon on a foggy night.

She said to Adam, "I was talking to T.P. He's back at school, you know." Her voice squeaked. Dammit, she didn't want to sound wimpy, but her vocal cords were not in the mood to play the role of a woman in control of her emotions.

"No, I didn't know," Adam said. "I've been busy talking to Detective Pontrelli about a new . . . development in the investigation."

Greta's eyes shifted from Adam back to Pontrelli. What in hell was going on? She said, "I don't understand."

Pontrelli removed his elbow from the top of the file cabinet.

"Well, we've been looking for a gang connection, or a love connection with these kids and their boyfriends. Anything to tie the murders of the two girls together."

"That part I understand."

"What I'm trying to say is, I've been going in the wrong direction. I've got to step back from these kids and look at the bigger picture." Pontrelli apparently was not accustomed to admitting he had made a mistake. His face had taken on the color of wet cement.

Greta sat down opposite Adam's desk, but Adam was not looking in her direction. She turned to Pontrelli. "But what about Rudy Smith? Aren't you still looking for him?"

Pontrelli said, "Nope. That's the new development. Smith turned up about five-thirty this morning. Your custodian bought himself a new car, and it looks like he was thinking about leaving town."

Greta said, "So did you arrest him?"

Pontrelli shook his head.

Adam spoke up. "Tell her, for God's sake."

"Tell me what? Why didn't you arrest Rudy?"

Pontrelli sighed. " 'Cause he wasn't going anywhere. He took a couple of real hard ones on the back of his head. Probably never knew what hit him."

Greta's eyes widened. "You mean Rudy is dead?"

"They don't get any deader."

23

THE blood drained from Greta's head. A floating feeling had moved in where her feet used to be. "Rudy was murdered?" Her voice sounded tinny in her own ears. She didn't expect an answer; she just needed time until the words registered in her mind, until a synapse finally connected.

Pontrelli said, "Yeah, your whole theory just went down the drain."

"Where did you find him?"

"Not too far from here. Over by the on-ramp to the Five. My guess is he was waiting there for somebody before getting on the freeway and heading out of town."

"You said he bought a new car."

Adam said, "Greta, there's no need for you to upset yourself with the details."

She bit her lip. Adam's apparent concern made tears rise, stinging behind her eyes, but she fought them back. "No, Adam, I want to know." She turned to Pontrelli. "The car?"

"Smith was lying on the ground next to a three-year-old Corvette. Had the sales slip in the glove compartment. Paid cash."

"How much?"

"Twenty grand."

Greta sucked in air through her teeth. "Then he *was* blackmailing the killer. I was right!"

Pontrelli raised his eyebrows. "Let me guess. You have another theory."

Greta no longer felt disconnected from her extremities. In fact, now that Rudy's role in all this finally made sense, she felt a sudden charge of energy. "Yes, don't you see?"

"Sure, I see what you're driving at, but we're still short a couple of things, like suspects and motives."

Greta ignored the barb in Pontrelli's tone of voice. "Rudy quit his job and went to buy a Corvette all in the same day. Not a coincidence. Rudy must have extorted the money for the car from the killer. Then maybe Rudy got greedy, wanted more money, perhaps a steady bankroll, but the killer wasn't willing to be blackmailed, so he had to kill Rudy, too."

Adam chuckled and covered his mouth with his hand. "Greta, you watch too much television. That's pretty far-fetched, isn't it, Detective Pontrelli?"

"No more than the theory you came up with when we were talking earlier," Pontrelli answered.

Greta could have kissed Pontrelli. "Adam, you didn't tell me you had a theory."

Blue veins bulged on Adam's temples. A flush tinged his face. "Well, I didn't actually until I heard that Rudy had been killed. I asked Detective Pontrelli what he thought about the possibility of a psychopath. I thought it might be someone who had nothing but trouble when he was a kid in high school. Maybe this guy somehow transferred his anger onto this campus, and decided to seek his revenge through random acts of violence, striking out at, so to speak, his past."

Greta shook her head. "I don't think there was anything random about it. And your theory doesn't explain how Rudy fell into enough cash to buy a Corvette on the very day he quit his job."

Pontrelli said, "Maybe he won the lottery?"

Adam smiled and then broke into a short laugh, apparently enjoying the way Pontrelli had just rescued him from Greta's theory. It was a nasty laugh, one that she had never heard from Adam before. Her fear that Adam might be involved in this whole mess once again reared its ugly head. She had to ask him about his talk with Belinda, when Belinda reported Rudy's advance, but she didn't dare do it in front of Pontrelli.

No matter how hard she tried not to think about it, her suspicions began to do battle with the love she felt for Adam. A lump the size of a varsity football twisted in her gut.

Pontrelli said, "You two armchair detectives can sit around jawing about your theories for the rest of the day if you want, but I gotta get back to work. Remember, we still don't have the killer. Smith didn't pound the back of his own skull into chopped liver; somebody did it for him.

"And we also have to remember the note you got yesterday, Mrs. Gallagher. There were no prints we could lift from the paper besides yours, and the handwriting didn't jibe with the handwriting on Smith's letter of resignation. Of course, with a scribble like that, he could have written your note with his left hand. If Smith sent the note, you can rest easy. But if Smith's killer sent the note, you got a problem."

"That's right," Adam said, his voice unusually loud. "I had almost forgotten about the note. I insist you give Greta some kind of protection."

"I'll see what we can do. I've already increased police protection on campus. Double what we had yesterday, and I'll get a couple of uniforms to spend the night outside your house. Do I have your address?"

While Pontrelli flipped through his notes looking for Greta's address, she repeated it for him. A couple of uniformed police officers outside her door tonight sounded like a good idea.

A chime, almost like a doorbell, signaled that someone was about to make an announcement over the public address system.

A male voice came over the speaker in Adam's office. "May I have your attention, please?" It was Leonard Irving, the eleventh grade counselor. "Will all teachers please escort your students to the library at once? Counselors will meet with the student group in the library. Teachers should report to the Oral Arts room for a staff meeting. I repeat, pupils to the library, teachers to the Oral Arts room. Today will be a minimum day for pupils and faculty; dismissal will be at twelve twenty-one. Students on the school lunch program will be served lunch as usual, but regular cafeteria service has been canceled."

Pontrelli said, "I'm glad you're finally taking my advice and putting all the kids in one place. You follow through with my instructions for the school's closure?"

Adam's face reddened again. This was the first Greta had heard about officially closing the school. It seemed there was more than one thing Adam hadn't told her.

Adam said, "I'm waiting for the final go-ahead from the superintendent, but I'm certain he'll get back to me within the hour. Parents have been screaming all the way up the ladder to the mayor. One father even telephoned the governor."

"Good," Pontrelli said. "I don't want anyone but cops and security guards on this campus after today."

Adam nodded without answering.

"What about the crisis hot line and the support center we headquartered up in the counseling office?" Greta asked. "A lot of our kids still need help."

Pontrelli shook his head. "They also need to be alive. I don't want anyone wandering around the campus. Too many places for the killer to hide."

Greta said, "What if we tell the students to come in the front gate and to report directly to the office?"

Pontrelli rubbed his left temple with his fingertips. "Tell you what, let me set up a room over at the Foothill Station for you people to counsel kids. At least there the counselors and the kids will be safe."

Greta nodded her agreement. There didn't seem to be any point in arguing with Pontrelli's decision. Besides, Pontrelli seemed pleased she was willing to give up the support center on campus. He nodded to them and got up and left the office without another word. She was finally alone with Adam.

Greta stood up and turned to him. Her questions about Belinda burned in her mind, but she couldn't get the words off the tip of her tongue. She couldn't do it. What if she was entirely wrong? She could blow her chances of a relationship with Adam with her wild accusations. Instead, she said, "I'll go help in the library."

Adam said, "The other counselors can handle it if you'd rather go home. I can meet you at your place later, and we'll have lunch."

"You seem to forget, I don't have a car. I spent the night at your place, remember?" Tears crept back into the corners of her eyes.

"Of course," Adam said. "You can tell how much I've got on my mind, can't you?"

"I guess we're all on overload."

"So we'll go for lunch after dismissal, and I'll drive you back to your car."

Greta went to the door. "I have a lot of phone calls to make, so I may have to hang around here for a while. Let's skip the lunch idea. Maxine can always drive me over to your place to pick up my car."

Adam looked wounded, as if she had just slapped him. "Okay," he said, "I'll see you later."

Greta was out the door before Adam could make further plans. The library, even though it meant a morning of trying to deal with confused, scared teenagers, sounded like a good place to be. She hadn't embarrassed herself by hinting that Adam was involved in murder, at least not yet. She hadn't even suggested he had withheld an important bit of information from the police. So whatever feelings Adam had for her remained intact.

But that same black thought hung over her like the rain clouds hung over the school. What if Adam actually was the older man in Belinda's life? If Greta didn't somehow learn the truth, she might find herself sleeping with a killer.

Fewer than ninety pupils were milling about inside the library when Greta walked in. Fran Elliot, the other senior counselor, was busy dividing the group into grade levels so each counselor could work with his or her regular counselees, but Fran soon discovered that most of the kids were seniors. She threw up her hands and told each counselor to randomly take fifteen or so pupils to a spot where they could talk.

Greta led eighteen seniors, mostly kids she already knew, to a table in a far corner. The kids wanted to talk, but some were so frightened their words didn't quite make sense. When she told them how the search for the custodian had ended, two girls began to cry. Their worries shifted, almost instantaneously, from concern over the girls who had been killed to fear of what might happen next, who the next victim might be. Then there was the practical worry about how a disruption in the school year could affect their graduation.

"We'll never be able to graduate in June if the school is closed," one girl said.

Another said, "I've got to have Algebra to get into college, but only eight kids showed up for class today, so we didn't go into the next chapter. Besides that, all we do in class is talk about the murders."

Greta said, "Talking about what has happened is good

therapy for all of us. You'll have time to make up the course work after they catch the killer."

"What if they don't catch him?" one boy said. "Can they keep McCormick closed if they don't catch him?"

"Well," Greta answered, "I don't know. I, for one, have faith the killer will somehow slip up and give himself away. They'll catch him."

"Haven't you ever watched 'Unsolved Mysteries' on TV?" Greta shook her head.

The boy went on. "Sometimes killers dodge the cops for years and years before they get caught. Some don't ever get caught."

Greta searched the faces of the young men and women sitting around the huge table. The fear in their eyes told her that someone had to catch this maniac, whoever he was, before he struck again, and she had to do her part. Adam had withheld information from the police and now she was doing the same. Maybe it was up to her to encourage Adam to tell them what he knew. Maybe she had to do it for him. Granted, Pontrelli and Zamora and all the other police officers were working overtime, but their main concern was to clean up a nasty mess on the police blotter. Greta had a bigger stake in solving the crime.

If Adam was involved, he had gone to some pretty desperate lengths to tie up loose ends so far. How long would he permit Greta to stumble about until she unearthed a clue that could connect him to the murders? She had to learn the truth. She had permitted her own pain to cloud her logic. So what if Adam had betrayed her? She could recover from a few lies intended to get her into bed, couldn't she?

Gradually, the students in the library left for home. At eleven-fifteen, the library phone rang, and Fran called to Greta.

"It's for you. The police."

Greta picked up the phone. "Hello."

"That you, Greta? Pontrelli here."

Greta noted that Pontrelli had used her first name. He sounded like this was something *really* urgent. "Yes," she said quickly.

"Is the Bench kid on campus with you? Someone said he had shown up for school today."

"He was here earlier, but I think he went home. What's wrong?"

Pontrelli said, "I'm gonna have to pick him up again. Something new turned up."

"What is it?"

Pontrelli hesitated, then said, "Listen, I want you to keep this under your hat, okay? This is something I'm not even giving to the press just yet."

"Sure, of course."

"It's the preliminary lab report. They checked the Corvette and the other stuff in Smith's possession. I thought things were pretty deep, but this case must go halfway to China."

Greta was afraid to put her thoughts into words, but she had to know. "What does this have to do with T.P.?"

Pontrelli's voice was rough, like a clap of thunder over the phone. "Remember I told you we found a receipt for Smith's car in the glove compartment?"

"Yes," she said.

"Receipt was in an envelope. The envelope had T.P. Bench's fingerprints all over it."

24

THREE boys remained in the library, pretending to browse through the current affairs section. They didn't seem to be together, yet they hovered close to one another. Their need to somehow stay in touch with the familiar routine of school saddened Greta, but the situation was out of her hands. A few minutes earlier Adam had announced to the students and teachers that McCormick High would be closed until further notice. Just like that. Temporary accommodations would eventually be set up to provide an educational program, but where and when was still unknown.

This news on top of Pontrelli's bombshell about T.P.'s fingerprints showing up in Rudy's car didn't do much for her anxiety level. She had believed T.P.'s story. She had believed in him. Well, so much for her insights, so much for her great counselor's ability to "know" these kids like the back of her hand.

What had T.P. been doing with Rudy just a few hours after his release from Juvenile Hall? How was the kid involved in this whole mess to begin with? T.P. and Rudy together, for any reason, just didn't make sense. God, she needed some answers.

Then there was Adam. Maybe she had jumped to conclusions about Adam's withholding information. His forgetting that Belinda had told him about Rudy's advance was minor when compared to the tremendous pressures Belinda's murder had created for Adam. The police, the school board, the parents, the press, everyone held Adam responsible. Greta felt guilty, but only when she wasn't feeling betrayed.

She said good-bye to one of the lingering boys who finally decided to go home, and then started for the door herself. Her legs felt heavy, as if she were plowing through water in the shallow end of a swimming pool.

Greta stepped outside the library into the rain. She walked toward the counseling office, thinking, trying to rearrange the facts in this puzzle so something, anything, about the three murders made sense. Nothing did. She had to talk to Adam right away or else she was going to drive herself crazy worrying about it.

She glanced across the pavement puddled with little lagoons of rainwater toward the parking lot in front of the school. At least three brightly painted television vans overshadowed the cars. That meant at least three crews with their Minicams and microphones were vying to be the first to broadcast the story about the school's closure. She guessed she wouldn't be able to speak to Adam privately for at least an hour.

The rain had let up a little, but dark clouds boiled on the horizon to the west. The rest of the storm, perhaps the worst part of it, was on its way. She went the long way around the administration building, avoiding the dry indoor corridor, which was probably overrun with TV crews. She let herself into the far end of the building, the entrance closest to her own office. Sure enough, the television people swarmed at the other end of the hall, stabbing microphones into Adam's face.

She ducked into the counseling office, hoping the reporters hadn't spotted her. Vera was busy on the phone. Fran Elliot was talking to a group of six red-faced seniors at the far end of the room. Three heads were visible through the window in Greta's office door. All the other counselors' doors were closed. They thought their support center had experienced a lot of business this past week, but Greta was certain what they had seen so far was just the tip of the iceberg. Young people might bounce back from tragedy faster than older ones in general, but a lot of these kids would carry around some pretty heavy baggage as a result of the three murders for years to come.

When she opened her door, the three people inside her office jumped to their feet. Wendy Yoshimura and her parents.

Greta forced a weak smile. "I hope you haven't been waiting long."

Wendy looked terrible, her once sassy, headstrong manner replaced by tearful brooding. The puffiness around her eyes made her appear almost slow-witted. Mrs. Yoshimura, as short as Wendy but much thinner, had wrung the handkerchief between her fingers into a taut rope. Mr. Yoshimura bowed slightly in Greta's direction. His thinning black hair was slicked straight back from a high forehead.

"Ms. Gallagher," Wendy said between sniffles, "I'm checking out of school."

Greta was not entirely surprised. Wendy would probably be the first of many withdrawals. "Where will you go?" she asked, gesturing for them to sit down again.

"L.A. Baptist High has accepted me, subject to verification of my grades."

"Are you certain that's what you want?" Greta asked, knowing the decision had probably come from her parents. "L.A. Baptist will be quite different from a public school."

Mrs. Yoshimura continued to twist the handkerchief. Mr. Yoshimura looked straight ahead at the wall behind Greta. Greta guessed he was not very fluent in English.

Wendy nodded. "Even if they caught the killer today, I couldn't go to school here ever again. My two best friends died here."

"I know," Greta said, "and I understand. I just meant you

179

might feel more at home in another public high school rather than a private school."

"I don't care about that. All I want is to get the credits I need to get into college." Wendy looked at her father out of the corner of her eye. "You can give us a copy of my records, can't you?"

The plea in Wendy's eyes convinced Greta she had no choice. "Sure, no problem," Greta said. "You just wait right here; I'll be back in a moment."

Greta pulled Wendy's cumulative record from the file cabinet and carried it over to the copier machine. The good students wouldn't wait around for whatever makeshift program the school board and Adam would concoct. Those who could afford private school would take that route. If McCormick High ever went back into business, they'd be left with a totally different makeup in their student body. Wendy's departure was only the beginning of a mass exodus.

She slid the Xerox copies of Wendy's transcript into a large envelope and sealed it with a white stick-on label. Over the label, she rubber-stamped the school's name and address. Not much of a security system, but it would make L.A. Baptist High confident the grades had not been altered.

She handed the envelope to Wendy. "Here's everything you'll need for now. We'll mail the entire folder when we hear you've been accepted officially. Good luck, Wendy."

Wendy choked back tears for a moment, then rushed into Greta's arms. Mrs. Yoshimura looked on, apparently shocked at her daughter's breach of propriety, while Mr. Yoshimura averted his eyes completely. Greta hugged Wendy, wanting desperately to say something that would make the girl's pain go away. The words just didn't come.

"Bye, Ms. Gallagher," Wendy said finally.

"Good-bye, Wendy. When this is all over, try to come back

and visit me, let me know how you're doing at the new school. Promise?"

"I'll try."

Greta shook hands with Mrs. Yoshimura, pressing too hard against the woman's polite but frail grip. Mr. Yoshimura bowed again, both hands straight down along his sides. Greta bowed her head toward him, not certain bowing was the right thing to do. Mr. Yoshimura backed out of Greta's tiny office, then turned and walked toward the exit, his family following behind him. For about the hundredth time today, Greta wanted to cry.

She gazed out the window. The sharp edges of the window-panes seemed to blur, growing softer in the dying light. In the distance, the sky seethed, now an even darker blanket of gray, but it didn't seem to be raining more than a drizzle at the moment. Still, there was no doubt a real downpour was on its way. She heard footsteps and a rustling of paper coming up behind her. She spun around.

"You look like shit," Maxine said, juggling two white paper bags in one hand, an umbrella in the other.

"Thanks," Greta said. "I love you, too."

"I brought food, and I don't want to hear any crap about fast food being junk, garbage, fattening, or immoral. You can't go on and on like this without eating something, and I don't have time to bake whole-wheat bread and raise a crop of alfalfa sprouts."

"Okay, you win. I guess right about now I could use a Jewish mother."

Maxine unpacked the food, lining up the containers by twos on Greta's desk. Little grease-stained paper bags held orders of French-fried zucchini and onion rings. Next came barbecued chicken sandwiches, packed in flimsy cardboard boxes, and two milkshakes, chocolate, frozen into a permanent icy sludge. In spite of everything her head told her, the heavy aroma of barbecue sauce and onion reminded Greta she was starving. She glanced at her watch. It was one-fifteen, hours since she had eaten a slice of toast and sipped a cup of coffee with Adam.

"Thanks," Greta said. "We'll probably both die of clogged arteries."

"Around here, that sounds like a good deal. Besides, this is no time to torture ourselves with good nutrition." Maxine removed her raincoat and settled into a chair with the usual clanking of bracelets and bobbing of earrings. "I've been on the phone for two hours, trying to find out what this school closure does to us pay-wise."

Greta sat down at her desk facing the food and Maxine. "I hadn't thought about our paychecks. What do you think will happen?"

Maxine crunched into a wedge of fried zucchini and chewed. "School board wants us to tote barges up and down the L.A. River to make up for lost teaching time, but our old contract has us covered. I'll bet that becomes a bargaining chip if they ever get around to offering us a new contract."

"So we get full pay even if we don't work?"

"Not exactly. We have to serve hours in another school or in this makeshift deal they've dreamed up. Did you hear they want us to meet our classes at Mission College? That's one helluva walk for most of the kids."

Greta shrugged. She was preoccupied by the unaccustomed taste of the overly sweet, thick shake even though it was almost impossible to suck through the straw. She tried to remember when she had last pigged out on one of these; probably not since the first few weeks after her separation from Carl. The prospect of divorce had sent her on a real junk food binge, trying to bury her depression under a buffer of sugar.

Greta stopped struggling with the shake and her guilt for a moment and looked at Maxine. "Maybe Mission College was the only facility available."

"Maybe the assholes didn't try very hard. Those jerks on

the school board won't have to walk five to ten miles to school, so what do they care?"

"I guess it won't be for long."

Maxine wiped her mouth with a stiff paper napkin. "Yeah. By the way, did you ask Adam about the thing between Belinda and Rudy?"

"Not yet, I haven't had a chance." Greta kept her eyes on the foamy bubbles rimming the edge of the milkshake cup. She didn't enjoy lying to Maxine. "But I did talk to Pontrelli on the phone."

"Yeah?" Maxine looked at her, waiting for the rest of it.

"Keep this to yourself. It's something I'm not supposed to talk about."

"You know me and secrets. It'll go with me to my grave, which I hope won't be too soon."

Greta looked into the outer office to make certain no one was in earshot. Vera stood talking to another counselor at the far end of the room. "Pontrelli told me the lab found T.P.'s fingerprints on an envelope in Rudy's car. It doesn't make any sense at all."

"No kidding? Wouldn't that mean T.P. got in touch with Rudy almost instantly after he was released from Juvie?"

"It appears that way," Greta said.

"Shit. I wouldn't have guessed T.P. had anything to do with the conspiracy."

Greta stopped chewing. "Conspiracy. That's an odd choice of words, isn't it?"

"I don't know. You've got two girls strangled, Rudy looking like he might have done at least one of them, and then he gets killed, Adam withholding information, and now T.P.'s fingerprints where they're not supposed to be. What would you call it?"

"I don't know," Greta said with a sigh, "but I guess it's time I go have that little talk with Adam."

183

25

GRETA tossed the last of her food wrappers from lunch into the wastebasket. "Thanks for the food, Max. Are you going to hang around here much longer?"

Maxine stood up, fluffing her hair with an automatic gesture of her right hand. "I want to see if I can find out whether we're moving to Mission College for sure. If so, I'll get busy on my requisitions for next week."

"What do you need?"

"A ton of art supplies, and if I don't have the district deliver new stuff, I'll have to schlepp whatever I can scrounge around here."

"Well, when you're finished, I may need a ride to my car," Greta said.

"Where's your car?"

"In Adam's garage."

Maxine shook her head. "The next thing I know, I'll be making teeny little cucumber sandwiches for a goddamn bridal shower."

Greta didn't even feel like responding to that one. "Can you take me?"

"Sure, no problem. I'd like to get a look at this lavish palace you've been telling me about anyway. I'll check back here when I'm finished with my order. You'll be in the office, won't you?"

"Yeah, after I've had a chance to track down Adam."

The odor of fried grease lingered in Greta's cubicle long after Maxine left. Greta sat there, thinking about what she would say to Adam. Rehearsing wasn't going to make it any easier. She just had to do it.

She walked down the corridor to the main office. Two of the hallway's overhead lights had burned out, leaving the area dark and shadowy, and the main office had been abandoned by the clerical staff as well as the teachers. Even dependable Old Faithful Connie was gone. Weird, but it wasn't the usual afterhours kind of emptiness, but more like walking into the old one-room schoolhouse in a ghost town. The door to Adam's office stood open. Apparently the television crews had gotten their scoops and gone off to patch together the bits and pieces into a news segment.

"Adam," she called, approaching his door. Adam did not answer, but she could see that the light was on. She stuck her head through the doorway and looked around. Adam sat hunched over his desk, his forehead resting on one fisted hand.

"Adam? Are you all right?"

He jerked upright, quickly lowering his arm. Red indentations from his fingers remained on his forehead. "Oh, Greta. Come on in."

She walked over to his desk. "I see the TV people have gone."

"For now. They'll be back."

"I hear we're moving to Mission College."

Adam pushed his chair away from the desk. One of the little round casters on the legs of the chair squeaked. "I'm afraid it's out of my hands. The superintendent wants instruction to go on as usual. He selected Mission College and made all the arrangements."

"I see," Greta said, walking over to the window. A gentle splatter of rain once again ticked against the glass. She felt much

185

too nervous to say what she had to say, but she wasn't going to chicken out this time. She swallowed over the lump in her throat. "Adam, there's something I want to ask you."

"Fire away."

Greta went to the chair opposite Adam's desk and sat facing him. The width of the desk seemed like a great wooden barrier separating them by miles. She cleared her throat. "I heard that Rudy Smith made a pass at Belinda shortly before her death. Belinda reported this to you, didn't she?"

Adam's expression turned hard, but tiny gray pools of moisture accumulated in the corners of his eyes. "Who told you this?"

"That doesn't matter," she answered. "Why didn't you tell Detective Pontrelli?"

Adam lowered his eyes, as if her words had slashed into his flesh. "I had forgotten all about it. I didn't think it was significant."

She tilted her head, looked at him doubtfully. "You didn't?"

"I get complaints all the time, Greta. Girls complain that teachers look down their blouses, that boys look up their skirts. Gym teachers are supposed to have hidden cameras in the girls' shower room, the rest rooms have peepholes, for God's sake. You wouldn't believe how much of that kind of stuff goes through their minds."

"But Belinda complained, and then she was murdered, wasn't she?"

"True. And when Pontrelli questioned me about the men on the staff, I honest-to-God forgot. I never thought of Belinda's complaint about Rudy until you brought up his name to Pontrelli and Pontrelli questioned me about him."

So Pontrelli wasn't sleepwalking half the time after all. Greta said, "And even then you didn't tell him?"

Adam took a deep breath, let it out again in a rush. The color had left his face and suddenly he looked almost unhealthy, like he had just gotten over a bad case of the flu. "I guess you caught me on this one. I didn't tell Pontrelli because I was embarrassed I had forgotten, and then as the case progressed, I thought . . ."

"What did you think?"

"Greta, I don't know what I thought. With so much pressure coming at me from every direction, I guess that one little detail just got away from me. The parents, the police, even the damned reporters just never let up. It was like I never had a minute's peace, except for those wonderful hours I spent alone with you."

Greta clenched her teeth. She wasn't going to let him pull her into his whitewash with more of his sweet talk. "Adam, if you had spoken up, Pontrelli might have clued in to Rudy a bit earlier. Your information could have saved Irene, maybe even Rudy."

Adam stood and began pacing. This nervous habit had become damned irritating, like watching a trapped fly frantically bouncing back and forth between the walls in her tiny bathroom at home. She never could understand why it didn't just fly into a larger room.

Adam said, "Don't you think I haven't thought of that about a million times since we found Irene? I keep telling myself Irene would have died anyway, that Rudy didn't kill her, but the fact that I neglected to tell the police what I knew will haunt me for the rest of my life."

"Or until we know who *really* killed Irene."

Adam turned and stared at her. Little beads of sweat had formed on his upper lip. "Don't tell me you think Rudy was innocent? Even after he used the dental appointment as a phony alibi?"

"Oh, he covered his tracks all right, but we can't be certain he murdered Irene. Maybe he went to the dentist's office, sneaked back on campus, and then observed someone *else* killing her. Rudy wasn't in this alone. He was blackmailing somebody, and that somebody killed him."

Now Adam's face drained completely. "Who do you think did it?"

Greta's patience with Adam's feigned naïveté was wearing thin. "Who else but the father of Belinda's baby?"

Adam walked over to where she sat. "Then you really don't know?"

"Let's just say I have my suspicions."

"Have you told Pontrelli your suspicions?"

Greta didn't like the look in his eye, and she didn't like the way he was fishing to see how much she knew. "We talk. We talked on the phone just a few minutes ago."

"I suppose you told him about the error I made?"

"No, Adam. You can tell him about it yourself, not that it matters now."

Adam took her hands in his and pulled her to her feet. "It matters only if you think less of me because of it. You want the truth?"

He was squeezing her hands a bit too tightly. "I'd love the truth," she said.

Adam looked down, studying their clenched fists. "When you discovered Belinda, what was the first thing that ran through your mind?"

"I don't know. I was horrified. Belinda, lying there dead. It was terrible."

"You thought about Belinda then?"

"Of course. She had her whole life ahead of her, and just like that, it was over."

Adam relaxed his grip on her slightly. "You know what I thought about when I walked into the workroom and saw her body on the floor?"

He looked her in the eyes. She shook her head. A sinking feeling deep in her gut pressed against a nerve she didn't even know she had. Why did she suddenly think yesterday's fantasy of Adam and Greta going off into the sunset and living happily ever after was about to shatter?

Adam said, "I thought about myself. What this would do to my career. How it would kill my chances of moving up the ladder into one of the deputy superintendents' offices. That's what I'd really like to do, you know."

"Why? You seem to have more than enough money." Greta was immediately sorry she had kicked him when he was down, but perhaps even that didn't matter anymore. Her hero had feet of clay and the rest of him had been carved out of some pretty superficial stuff as well. Greta chewed on the insides of her cheeks to hold back the tears.

Adam said, "Money isn't the reason you seek a job like that."

"What is the reason?" she asked. "You like the idea of the power, prestige, or what? Maybe someday you might work your way up to superintendent?"

Adam broke into a crooked grin. His forehead was now veiled with little pearls of sweat. It couldn't be that warm in the room, yet Greta felt it, too. Under her suit jacket, her sweater had fused to her skin.

He said, "I guess I've never broken it down into a specific reason, but I've had a need to do something important on my own for a long time. Something that had nothing to do with Helen or her money."

"Moving up the ladder in the district takes a bit of effort. Helen had nothing to do with your getting a principal's position, did she?"

Adam's expression turned flat, like he was looking not at her but at someone off at a great distance. "Helen wasn't impressed with my job, or rather I should say her family wasn't impressed with my line of work, but all that isn't important as far as you're concerned."

"What is?" Greta asked.

Adam sighed. "You found Belinda and you thought about the poor girl. When I saw her I thought about poor me. I didn't mean to turn it into a cover-up, but I kept my mouth shut about Belinda and Rudy because I didn't want to be personally connected in any way to the investigation."

Greta studied his eyes. A cold white light from the overhead fluorescents shone directly in his face. No question Adam was clearly in pain, but that didn't mean he was telling her the whole story. Maybe Adam made a habit of circumventing the truth when it served his needs. She thought about last night. How much of what he had said during their lovemaking had been lies?

She spoke in a voice she could barely hear herself. "So, that's all there was to it? You were just trying to protect your job?"

"Believe me, Greta, I'll never make such a mistake again. I thought only of myself at first, but since then, every time I close my eyes, I see Belinda looking up at me from the floor, those eyes boring into me as if she were begging me to help her."

Greta's mind went numb. Every muscle in her body seemed to tighten at once. Adam could not have seen Belinda's eyes unless he had been in the room sometime before Greta found the girl. Hadn't she closed Belinda's eyes herself, long before Adam arrived on the scene?

Greta stared at the man she thought she loved, gooseflesh racing up and down her arms. A thousand needles punctured her brain. This could mean only one thing.

Adam had killed Belinda.

26

GRETA'S heart jackhammered up into her throat. She held her breath. She had to think, get control of herself. Now was a good time to remember all the clever things she said to hysterical kids when they jumped to conclusions. Consider the alternatives.

Maybe Adam wasn't the actual killer. Sure, he was involved somehow, but what if this was yet another cover-up? Maybe Adam had stumbled onto someone else strangling Belinda. But who? Rudy? T.P.? No matter how incriminating the evidence, she still didn't believe that T.P. was capable of murder, and why would Adam be willing to put his neck on the line to cover up for T.P.? The fingerprints proved that T.P. was involved with Rudy, but where did Adam fit in?

One thing was certain, Adam hadn't killed Rudy, because he had never left his bedroom last night. Thoughts of last night zoomed through her mind like a video on fast forward. God, don't let Adam be a killer. How could she have fallen totally, desperately, in love with a murderer?

Adam let go of her hands and ran his fingers up her arms, resting them on her shoulders. Greta stiffened, afraid to dash for the door, yet certain that's what she needed to do. Think, she told herself. He doesn't know I closed Belinda's eyelids. I never told him. He doesn't suspect a thing.

Adam's fingers crept toward her neck. He was murmuring

something, but the words were lost in the sound of her own blood roaring through the veins in her head, like a jet getting ready for takeoff. Adam's face was inches from her own, his bluish gray eyes black against the pasty white of his skin. Slowly, his fingers circled her neck, his thumbs resting gently on her throat. He pulled her closer.

He was going to kiss her!

"Nothing has changed between us," he said. He leaned forward and pressed his mouth against hers, freezing her lips somewhere just short of a scream.

Greta pivoted her whole body to one side, and Adam's hands abruptly fell away from her. He hadn't tried to strangle her; he had, instead, gently stroked the back of her neck with his fingertips, but fear had closed her throat nonetheless. It was torture just being near Adam, remembering the intense electricity of their lovemaking.

Maybe Adam couldn't help what had happened to Belinda, possibly even Irene. Maybe he was crazy, a psycho. But until she knew the truth, she had to get away from him. She needed time to think and time to call the police. Let Pontrelli figure out whether Adam was a crazed killer.

"You're upset, aren't you?" Adam said. He turned away from her, his shoulders stooping forward like a very old man. "I don't blame you. I'm disappointed with myself."

"No." Greta had found her voice, but it sounded strangely high-pitched to her own ears. "That's not it at all. What you did was perfectly natural under the circumstances." As she spoke, she edged toward the door. "I can't help it. I just feel uncomfortable kissing you right here in your office."

Adam looked as if he didn't believe that one. Not even for a second. "The campus is empty, except for the police. Let's get out of here. I'll drive you to my place to pick up your car."

"Oh, nuts," Greta said with a casual toss of her head, "I

forgot Maxine is probably standing in the rain waiting for me. I told her I'd meet her in the parking lot."

"She has enough sense to get inside her car, doesn't she? C'mon, we'll take my car and drive around to the faculty lot to look for her."

Greta had reached the open door. She grabbed the doorknob and yanked it open wider. No one was in the outer office. "Listen, why don't you wait right here for me? I have to run back to my office for my purse."

Adam moved closer. "I'll come with you." He grabbed her arm.

"Adam, you're hurting me."

He looked at his fingers clenched around her upper arm, but he didn't release his grip. A shot of pain flew all the way down to her fingertips.

"Just let me come with you," he said.

"No need," Greta said, pasting an artificial smile on her face. "I'll be right back after I make a stop at the ladies' room."

His hand fell away from her arm. "Just hurry," he said, "please."

Greta wanted to rub away the pain in her arm, but she didn't want Adam to know how much he had hurt her. If he would withhold evidence to save his job, would he kill her as well? She said, "I'll be back before you know it."

It looked as if he were going to let her go. Adam stared at her, his eyes watery and apologetic. If she were going to get away from him, now was her chance. She flashed him a weak smile and headed down the corridor toward the counseling office. A whole litany of do's and don't's stampeded through her head.

Don't tip him off by running. He'll hear footsteps echoing, he'll know. Be smart about this. Stay calm. The campus is crawling with police. All she had to do was find one of them and this whole nightmare would be over.

Greta reached the counseling office, which was now dark. Her purse was indeed in there, but the office had only one entrance. If Adam decided to follow her, she would be trapped. She walked to the exit at the end of the hall. She touched the panic bar on the door as delicately as she knew how, but the thing still rattled a hollow clunk that Adam must have heard even if he had remained inside his office. She slipped outside and eased the door shut. All the while, she kept checking the corridor through the pane of glass in the door for signs of Adam. The coast was clear.

It was still raining. Of all days, it had to be raining on this one.

She scanned the walkway for a police officer or one of the school's security people. No one was around. They were probably inside somewhere, taking shelter from the weather. She couldn't see another human being anywhere. Where would they be? Dammit, she should have phoned the police from the counseling office. Too late for that now; no way was she going back inside the building.

The leaden gray sky made it seem much later in the day than it was. Could the police have gone off duty already? No, she reasoned. The cafeteria was closed, but they could still make coffee in one of the two teachers' lounges. She would find half the police force gathered around a pot of hot coffee. She half ran, half walked toward the nearest lounge, trying to avoid the puddles. Somewhere behind her, she heard a door slam. Her heart jumped. Adam had heard her leave the administration building. He was coming after her.

Maxine's classroom was slightly closer than the closest lounge. If Maxine was there writing her requisitions, Greta would have help. Together they could track down the police on campus or find a phone. Maybe she should just scream bloody murder to get anyone to rush to her aid. But what if Adam were the only one to respond?

She dashed around the corner of the art building to Maxine's room. Both doors were locked, but she hammered on one with her fist anyway. No light shone through the windows, and all logic told Greta that Maxine would not be bumbling around the room in the dark. Back to the lounge idea. Even if no police officers were taking a break in the lounge, the lounge had a phone.

She broke into a high-heeled jog, silently damning the person who had first dreamed up this design for women's shoes. The sound of her heels tapping against the concrete reverberated like shots from a machine gun. Adam would know exactly where she was headed. She leaned over and ripped off her shoes, recoiling from her first contact with the icy-cold, wet concrete in her stocking feet. She broke into a run.

Finally, puffing and short of breath, she reached the door to the lounge. A light shone through the frosted glass of the only window. She tucked her shoes under her arm, knocking with one hand and fumbling in her pocket for her school keys with the other. Somewhere on her key ring she had a key to the lounge. Her fingers trembled so badly she could hardly distinguish one key from another. She slapped against the door with the flat of her hand. No answer.

The key, yes, she had found the right one. Shivering, she thrust the key into the keyhole. Her heart was now thumping a steady drumbeat in her own ears. The lock finally gave way and the key turned to the right, but just then all of her senses froze.

Someone had come up from behind and placed a firm hand on her right shoulder.

27

GRETA spun around, bumping into him. She jerked backward, flinching from the slippery wetness of his vinyl raincoat. "For crying out loud, Stanley, what are you trying to do, give me a heart attack?"

Stanley's expression drooped nearly to his feet. "I called to you, but I guess you didn't hear me." He immediately pulled open the heavy door for her, like a child who was overly eager to help.

A quick look told her the police officers were not in the lounge. She ran to the phone.

"What's the matter with you?" Stanley asked, following her inside. "Why are you acting so jumpy? Why'd you take off your shoes?"

"Later." She dismissed Stanley's questions and turned her back to him. He didn't take the hint, but she didn't have time to worry about Stanley's hearing her conversation. She dialed Pontrelli's direct line.

The phone rang and rang until Greta thought the blood vessels in her ear would explode. She threw her shoes to the floor and forced her wet feet back into them. Her pantyhose had shredded, running up her legs in wide ladders. What little was left of her stockings squished water between her toes. Her feet stuck uncomfortably to the insoles of her shoes. Finally, she heard a click.

"Detective Zamora." The voice came loud and brusk.

Shit. Greta was hoping to speak directly to Pontrelli. "Is Detective Pontrelli in, please? This is Greta Gallagher over at the high school."

Zamora waited a second too long before responding. "He just stepped out. Is there something I can do for you?"

"I was just wondering . . ." This wasn't coming out right. She didn't want to sound stupid as well as hysterical. "I need help, but I can't talk about it over the phone. I'll explain it to Detective Pontrelli when he gets here."

Greta thought she heard Zamora issue a low snort. She could just see the smirk on Zamora's face.

"He's out, picking up the Bench kid for questioning. I'll try to get him on the radio if it's an emergency."

Stanley had meandered to the other side of the room, where he was casually examining a bulletin board that held yellowed notices of past importance and dog-eared cartoons. Greta had no doubt that Stanley could hear every word she said. She tried to whisper into the phone. "I have some important information about the case, but I'd rather explain it in person."

Zamora sighed. Not a heavy sigh, but enough of one to let Greta know she wasn't being taken seriously, or maybe Zamora was still pissed at her. "Okay," Zamora said, "I'll be right over, but you do know there's almost a dozen uniforms at the school, not to mention your own security people. You could explain your problem to one of them."

"Sure, if I could find them. This is a big campus, you know." Greta had raised her voice. Stanley lost interest in the bulletin board and walked back over to where she stood. "Just hurry, will you?" she added before she pressed the button to disconnect the call.

Greta dropped the receiver into its cradle. Stanley looked so confused she felt she owed him some sort of explanation, but how much could she tell him? She wouldn't even know where to begin. Stanley was not the first person she had thought of when she wanted to confide that she suspected her lover of murder. Stanley didn't even know she had a lover.

"Maybe I should go," Stanley finally said. "Unless there's something I can do to help."

"No, don't go," Greta practically shouted. "You can help me."

Adam's voice suddenly boomed into the room. "This is Adam Mason."

Greta almost jumped out of her soggy shoes. God, it was only the PA system. She had to get hold of herself.

Adam continued. "Will all school security and police officers please check into a disturbance at the north end of the P.E. field." He paused. "Greta Gallagher, please come to the main office."

His last words stitched into her brain. Surely by now Adam had discovered that Greta was not in the counseling office or the rest room, and he was probably ready to search every room in the school if he had to. She had to give him credit for remembering to do something about the police and the school security. Sending all of them scurrying to the most distant point of the campus was a clever move.

Greta said, "Stanley, will you go with me?"

"Where?"

Where indeed? Her car was at Adam's house, but her car keys were in her purse in the counseling office. Maxine was not in her classroom. Oh, my God. Maxine was somewhere on campus, possibly in Greta's office using the phone. But Adam had no reason to harm Maxine, did he? Unless—the thought kept recurring—Adam was crazy or psychotic. If that were the case, Maxine might be in as much danger as Greta.

Greta said, "I've got to find Maxine. She's around here somewhere."

Stanley shook his head. "I just saw her leave. She drove away with Fran Elliot."

"No," Greta insisted, "she wouldn't leave me here. She knew I was counting on her for a ride."

"They probably just went for doughnuts or something. They'll be back."

"Walk with me, Stanley. I have to find a cop, fast, and Adam just sent every one of them to the P.E. field."

"I can do better than that. We can use my car. I was loading up some math supplies, so it's right behind the building, parked in the service drive."

She could have kissed him. They hurried through the rain and up the three steps to the driveway that separated the main part of the campus from the physical education building and its adjoining fields. The clouds had finally let go, and a veritable downpour now cascaded into even deeper puddles all around them.

Stanley held the door of his car open for her and she dropped gratefully into a leather bucket seat in the red Mustang. The rain flew against the windows and pounded steadily against the car's exterior, but inside was warm and dry and had the smell of a brand-new car. She hadn't realized Stanley owned such a racy-looking car. Somehow she had always pictured him driving a ten-year-old clunker.

Stanley started the engine then, turning to her. "What are you so afraid of, Greta? Running into the killer?"

Stanley suddenly looked peculiar, almost rakish, as if taking the wheel of his flashy red car had given him a different personality. Another time or place and she probably would have laughed, but at the moment Stanley was all that protected her from Adam, and as much as she hated to admit it, she needed Stanley.

She blurted out, "Yes, in a way I *am* afraid of running into the killer, or at least one of the killers. There's more than one, you know."

Stanley raised an eyebrow and slid the automatic gearshift into Drive. He had the air of a teenager trying to impress chicks with his smooth moves. "You're something else, you know that? I think you've been working harder on this case than the cops."

Stanley drove to the end of the service drive and turned left to circle around to the far end of the P.E. field. He went about a half block, then pulled over next to a vacant lot that used to belong to a now-defunct boarding stable for horses. He shifted into Park.

Greta sat up straighter and peered through the raindrops pelting Stanley's side window. What little she could see from this distance seemed strangely out of focus, and now the windows had steamed up on the inside, practically obliterating any chance of her seeing what was happening across the field. "Not here, Stanley. I think I can see people over on the west side of the field. Drive to the corner and make another left."

But Stanley didn't drive anywhere. Instead, he turned sideways in his seat and faced her. His eyes narrowed before he spoke. "They're going to nail T.P. Bench for Belinda's murder, so why don't you give it a rest?"

Something unfriendly from her greasy lunch began to form little wads of lead in her stomach. Or maybe it was the tone of Stanley's voice that threw up the mental red flags. "Why do you say that?" she asked.

"The police have evidence that proves T.P. killed Rudy, so they'll figure out some way to tie him to Belinda's death even if T.P. wasn't the father of the kid she was carrying. It'll make a neat little package for the cops to hand over to the D.A., and then Pontrelli and his buddies can all congratulate themselves for being supercops."

A high-pitched noise whined inside Greta's brain. She almost expected a little light bulb, like you see in cartoons, to be glowing above her head. This was too incredible. Stanley's wife didn't understand him. He was a pathetic creature who desperately yearned for a little love and companionship, yet he also had a certain aura of vulnerability. The tormented victim, wronged by a shrewish wife, was appealing to some women. Maybe especially appealing to a very *young* woman. Why hadn't she tuned in to Stanley earlier?

"What about Irene?" Greta asked. "T.P. was in custody when she was killed."

Stanley grinned. "A witness who had been to scared to come forward when Rudy was alive is going to tell the police how Rudy grabbed Irene as she was walking between the bungalows and the next building. How Rudy knocked her silly with his fists before he strung my stolen necktie around her little neck. This witness will be the final piece to the puzzle the cops have been looking for."

Greta had a feeling she was on a free-fall from a very steep height. She said, "I guess it's safe to assume you are this reluctant witness."

"Yes, indeed," Stanley answered.

"But you were with me in the lunchroom."

"I was with you when Irene was *found*. There's a twenty-, thirty-minute difference the police will buy. After all, why would I lie?"

"But you didn't witness anything, did you?"

"Very good. I knew if you poked around long enough, you'd get lucky."

She had heard enough. Her brain ordered her to fling open the door and run, but it was almost as if she were paralyzed. Greta fingered the door latch with her right hand. Stanley watched her. She moved her knee, hoping her leg would conceal what she was doing.

"I don't think you want to do that," he said.

Her fingers froze around the latch as Stanley pressed a control, locking her door from the driver's side. Out of the corner of her eye she saw that the door lock buttons were the newer skinny kind that almost disappear into the upholstery when locked. The kind you can't get a hold on with a coat hanger—or your fingers.

"I'm really sorry you had to be so nosy—because I like you, Greta."

"The way you liked Belinda? I'll bet you liked her a lot."

Stanley's face went solemn. He said, "I've always thought there could be a very nice relationship between you and me if you'd only give me a chance. These sweet young girls are fine when you've got no one else, but with someone like you . . . Well, I guess there's no point going into it now, is there?"

Chills raced wildly over Greta's body, somehow all coming together at the base of her skull. She tried to steady her trembling knees with her left hand. "Belinda filled that empty space in your gut, didn't she? That place your wife doesn't quite reach?"

"See, that's what I mean," Stanley said, smiling. He wet his lips with his tongue. "You can see beyond the obvious. I guess I've been fooling around with adolescents so long I've forgotten how grown-ups think."

"I'm having a hard time visualizing you and Belinda . . ." It finally clicked. "Unless your position on the Scholarship Committee was some kind of lure."

Stanley grinned. "I happen to be *chairperson* of the Scholarship Committee. My decisions are usually rubber-stamped by the others. Cuts down on the time they have to spend at meetings."

"I guess I've underestimated you."

Stanley stared into her eyes. "The girls tell me I've also got a lot of animal attraction going for me."

Now at least she understood Belinda's reason for getting

involved with Stanley in the first place. Belinda had been too insecure to trust her own abilities.

Greta said, "But why'd you have to kill her, Stanley? Was she going to tell the world about your baby?"

Stanley nodded. "I told her to take precautions. She promised me she was on the pill."

"So Rudy saw you two argue? Did he see the actual murder? Is that why he blackmailed you?"

"That sleazy bastard crept around this place like a weasel. He saw enough to send me to the gas chamber, but he didn't care about that. He wanted money."

Greta blinked. "Which one of you sent me the threatening note? Rudy?"

Stanley laughed. "Rudy wasn't smart enough to think of anything original. I wrote it with my left hand, thought maybe I could get you to stop sniffing around. You're a boat rocker, you know that?"

Greta didn't know whether she should be angry or consider Stanley's need to get her off the case, so to speak, a compliment.

She said, "How did Irene fit in? Was she one of your girls, too?"

Stanley winced slightly. "C'mon, Greta, give me some credit. I never had more than one girlfriend at a time. Belinda and I connected last summer, in summer school."

"Irene knew something then?"

"Irene *thought* she knew something. Came to me, of all people, to report her suspicions before going to the police."

Stanley laughed. "She said *you* planted the idea in her head that Rudy might be involved, so Irene started pestering Rudy, asking him questions about Belinda."

Greta closed her eyes wishing she had kept her big mouth shut. Irene had tried to do the same kind of thing Greta had been doing. This wasn't the way it was supposed to work out.

Stanley went on. "Then she overheard Rudy bragging to

one of the other custodians about how he was going to find himself a brand new girlfriend. So Irene went right up to Rudy, bold as can be, and asked him if he killed Belinda."

"Which he denied, of course."

"Well, sure. But Irene didn't believe him. Told me so herself. Of course, she didn't know Rudy had just screwed me out of twenty thousand, which was why he thought he now had what it took to get a girlfriend." Stanley paused for a moment. "Irene would've gone to the police, too."

"But you warned Rudy and Rudy killed her," Greta added, shaking her head.

"Rudy never meant to kill her. He thought he could scare her into keeping quiet, but Rudy freaked out because Irene started to holler. He smacked her, knocked her senseless, then the dumb shit really panicked. He had swiped one of my neckties, of all things, to leave stuffed in her hand—to incriminate me as her attacker. Instead, he used it to finish her off."

"So next came Rudy. You had to get rid of him because of the blackmail, right?"

Stanley regarded her with an offhand shrug, bemused astonishment registering in his eyes. Like she should know the answer to that one without even asking.

"Of course," he said, "just like I have to get rid of you."

28

STANLEY'S right hand reached between the two seats into the rear of the car. He seemed to be groping for something on the floor.

Greta squeezed closer to the locked door. The strength had gone out of her legs; fear welded her to the seat. For an eternity she held her breath, her eyes fixed on Stanley's.

Finally, the air rushed from her lungs. "But I didn't witness any of this. You know I can't prove a thing."

"This is true, but I still can't have you sitting around discussing it with your friend Pontrelli, now can I?"

"You're forgetting your neat little package for the D.A. How will you blame my death on somebody else?"

Greta heard a rattle. Stanley had stopped fishing on the floor behind her and yanked something forward to the console between the two front seats. Greta recognized the familiar red-and-black gadget as a Gorilla, an automobile antitheft device used to lock the steering wheel when the car was parked. It looked heavy. It also looked clean, but perhaps the police crime lab could find traces of Rudy's blood on it. Maybe even a microscopic sample of a hair from the back of Rudy's crushed head.

"Your untimely death will be chalked up to the same confused kid who lost his cool and wasted Rudy," Stanley said. "Open the glove compartment."

Greta's fingers trembled, but she pushed the button that released the compartment. Stanley reached over her and pulled out a pair of clear plastic gloves. "It doesn't hurt to be thorough." He worked his hands into the gloves, wrenching the plastic over his knuckles.

Greta's time was running out. She needed a plan, but her mind wasn't registering anything that made sense. By the time she fumbled with the door lock button and pulled it up, Stanley could hammer her head into dog meat. The only advantage she seemed to have was Stanley's pride, his enjoyment in boasting about how ingenious he had been. If she could only keep him talking, telling his story all the way to the end, she might think of something to do.

"You know, Stanley, T.P. may be back in custody already, even as we speak," she said.

Stanley flexed his fingers and forced the air out of the gloves up to his wrists. "It doesn't matter. They'll find you in the foothills somewhere, under a pile of soggy leaves, and what with the rain, they won't be able to pinpoint the exact time of your death anyway. Besides, they'll find the kid's note."

Greta choked a tiny laugh. "You're not going to forge a confession from T.P.? That's not a smart move at all."

"Thank you, my dear, for recognizing a smart move when you see one."

Stanley reached into the glove compartment again, this time retrieving a white envelope. He handled the envelope delicately, by one corner, almost with the concern and precision of a surgeon excising a vital organ.

He removed a single sheet of paper from the envelope and held it up for Greta to see. "This little treasure is written in T.P.'s own handwriting, and his prints are all over it. Sort of a confessional."

Stanley read: "I know what I did is morally wrong, and I'm sorry. I know it's too late to change what I've done, but I promise I'll never do anything like this ever again. Signed, T.P. Bench."

Greta felt cold sweat running down her back. She noticed that Stanley had removed his foot from the brake pedal. "What did T.P. do? Chew gum in class?"

"Even worse. I caught him cheating on a test right about the same time I started having trouble with Belinda. I figured someday a confession from T.P. might come in handy. I even dictated what he should write." Stanley laughed out loud. "I told him if he ever so much as raised his eyes from his own paper during a test again, I'd give this to his folks. If he kept his nose clean, I promised to tear up the note."

Greta saw Stanley's hand go for the antitheft device. Her heart stopped beating. She whispered, "What did you do, get him to handle all your stationery so you could dump a whole series of crimes on the kid?"

While Stanley laughed at that one, Greta spotted two buttons above the armrest on her door. One had a *U* printed on it, the other an *L*. Of course! She hit the *U* to unlock her side and jerked open the door with her right hand, swinging her feet out into the rain. With her left hand, she yanked the gearshift down into one of the forward gears and then lunged headlong out of the car onto the ground.

Greta landed mostly on her knees, but somehow she scrambled to her feet and made a frenzied dash away from the car. This time she kicked off her shoes without bothering to pick them up and bolted down the street, heading back toward the school's service drive.

The rain sliced against her body in torrents. In moments she was soaked, sputtering as the downpour funneled into her open mouth when she screamed. She distinctly heard the squeal of Stanley's brakes behind her, followed by the slamming of a car door. Probably the one she had left open when she jumped.

A car came toward her from the other end of the long block, but it seemed to slow down in the middle of the street. She pushed herself harder; if she could only run close enough to the car so the driver could see she was being chased and hear her screams, she might have a chance. She heard the splat of Stanley's footsteps landing behind her. She didn't dare turn around to see how close Stanley was, but she was certain he was gaining on her.

Should she head for the weed-choked empty lot along the street to her left and try to cross to the houses beyond? No, the grass was probably littered with broken bottles. She was nearly blinded by the rain, but she didn't see anything on the street that might cut into her bare feet. Was she crazy, worrying about stepping on a piece of glass when Stanley was about to split open her skull? Her legs worked automatically, pumping against the tightness of her soaking-wet skirt.

She thought she heard shouting. Was Stanley yelling at her? Then a car horn blared. The car ahead was now speeding toward her. With the rain beating against her head and the tremendous pounding of her heart, all other sounds were a blur.

If she didn't stop soon, her lungs would surely explode, but she fought the pain, running harder, propelling herself away from Stanley. She could feel his presence towering behind her, getting closer and closer. Was that his hot breath on the back of her neck?

Then something hard and heavy plummeted between her legs from behind, cracking painfully against her ankles. Like a torpedo, she shot forward, her legs neatly pulled out from under her. Stanley had used the Gorilla to trip her. She felt the stinging fire of the road's surface biting deep into her hands and knees.

29

GRETA rolled over onto her back just in time to see Stanley raise his cumbersome weapon high above his head. From where she lay on the ground, Stanley looked like a giant, and she would have sworn he was grinning. She rolled again, frantically lurching to her knees and then struggled to her feet. The black-and-red Gorilla came pounding down, clanging against the wet blacktop just inches from where her head had been a second earlier.

The car raced up to them, squealing to a stop and fishtailing on the wet surface. The passenger's door flew open and Maxine screamed, "Get in!"

Greta vaulted into the car and slammed the door shut just as Stanley smashed the device against the side window. The glass splintered into a web of a million threads. She fumbled for the door lock, pushing the button down. Stanley took another swing and gouged the Gorilla through the network of broken lines, spraying Greta with a hailstorm of glistening pebbles.

Maxine stomped on the gas pedal, spinning her tires into a horrendous shriek until the tread finally dug in and the car tore away.

With her fingertips, Greta tried to assess the damage done to her face by the flying glass. She tasted blood, but then she remembered biting into her lip when she saw Stanley wielding his club above her head. Her ankles throbbed; her knees and the palms of her hands burned with pain, the reddened bruises seeping a trickle of blood. A piece of gravel was imbedded in her left knee.

"For God's sake," Maxine yelled above the roar of the engine, "you made me swallow my gum. What in hell's going on?"

Greta flicked away a piece of glass that had stuck dangerously close to her eye. "Stanley killed Belinda and Rudy. Rudy killed Irene."

"Holy shit, how'd you figure out all that?"

"Stanley told me the police would be able to prove T.P. killed Rudy. That meant Stanley knew they'd find T.P.'s fingerprints in Rudy's car even before Pontrelli released it to the news. After I guessed, Stanley told me everything, but then he had to kill me, too."

"Couldn't you just grade your fuckin' essays like all the other English teachers?" Maxine cried. "Oh, my God. He's after us."

Greta looked over her shoulder, out the rear window. The red Mustang hugged Maxine's bumper.

"Step on it," Greta cried. "Get away from him."

Maxine floored the gas pedal and spun around the corner toward the P.E. field. "I don't believe we're doing this, just like Thelma and Louise."

Stanley passed them on the left, grazing against Maxine's car, pushing her toward the curb. Metal ripped into metal. The screech was deafening. Maxine flew down the street, her two right tires bouncing off the curb every few feet, but somehow she kept the car under control. Then Stanley rammed his front fender into her left rear door, pushing them completely off the road and into a thicket of overgrown oleander.

A car sped toward them, and Greta leaned on Maxine's

horn. Whoever it was had to stop to help them. Stanley was now out of his car, bludgeoning his heavy steel gadget against the window on Maxine's side.

"Hold it right there, sucker," came a voice.

Greta looked past a stunned Maxine, through the grid of broken glass now radiating across her window, to see Detective Zamora holding her service revolver inches from Stanley's head. Stanley dropped the lock to the ground and held his hands high above his head, just like they used to do in the old cowboy movies.

Greta pushed open her door and ran around to Zamora. "He's the killer, at least one of them. Rudy killed Irene, but Stanley killed Belinda and Rudy."

Zamora looked unimpressed. "We'll get your statement, don't worry." She directed Stanley over to the hood of her unmarked police car. "Put your hands flat against the hood and spread 'em."

In a matter of seconds, Zamora had checked Stanley for concealed weapons and cuffed him. Damn, she's good at this, Greta thought. Greta turned and smiled at Maxine. Maxine opened her car door and crawled out, moaning.

"Are you okay?" Greta called, rainwater dripping off the end of her nose.

"Just ducky."

Two more cars, one a black-and-white, the other Pontrelli's came squealing up to Zamora's car.

Zamora said, "Why don't you two get in the back of my car out of the rain?"

Greta and Maxine hurried inside and slammed the doors behind them. Greta squeezed the water out of the hem of her skirt, leaving a puddle on the carpeted floor. She pulled off her soaked jacket and tossed it into the puddle. Her teeth chattered as she checked the swelling rising over her ankle bones. At least Stanley hadn't broken both of her legs, although he had probably meant to. Now, the pain in her knees and hands stung harder and harder. Greta shivered, chills ascending her back all the way to the roots of her hair.

Maxine took off her own raincoat and draped it blanket style over Greta, tucking the collar under her chin. "If you don't catch pneumonia, it'll be a miracle."

"My mother used to say that, thank you."

Maxine stared at Greta and shook her head. "Look at you! I've never seen such a mess. What the hell were you doing with Stanley in the first place?"

"I'll explain everything, but first, how did you know to come looking for me?"

"I went down to your office and bumped into Adam. He was really upset, acted like he had just gotten something crucial caught in his fly. He kept pacing like a caged animal and mumbled about you being 'out there' by yourself with a killer on the loose, and he should have gone with you."

"Then Stanley lied about your leaving campus with Fran," Greta said half to herself.

Maxine cast her a confused look. "I haven't seen Fran all day." She went on. "Then Adam begged me to check the ladies' room. I did, and when you weren't there, he said he bet you went up to the gym field to see what the disturbance was. That made him really crazy."

Greta closed her eyes and shook her head silently.

Maxine continued. "Pontrelli called in right after Adam made that announcement. The disturbance turned out to be Pontrelli cuffing T.P."

"Not again," Greta said.

"Yeah, well, T.P. was not looking forward to another weekend in Juvie, so he made a bit of a fuss. One of the gym teachers saw the commotion from a distance and called the main office. Is that where you were headed?"

"Max, I'm sure Adam isn't aware of this, but I took off

because of something Adam said. I was certain Adam had killed Belinda. I was looking for a cop."

Maxine wiped the steamy moisture from the side window with her hand. "No kidding? So what did Adam say?"

"He said he had seen Belinda's eyes when he went into the workroom after I found her. Max, I had closed her eyes myself before Adam arrived."

"So?"

"What do you mean, so? If he had seen her eyes open, I figured he had been there first."

Maxine said, "Unless her eyes opened again *after* you left the room. That happens."

Greta's eyes widened. "It does?"

Maxine grinned. "That's the first thing you should have learned in detective school."

"Don't be a such a smart ass. I'm serious."

"So am I. When my grandmother died her eyes kept blinking open no matter how many times my mother closed them. I was only fourteen, but I'll never forget it. Mom finally taped down her eyelids until the undertaker arrived."

"Oh, my God," Greta cried. "Max, I've really misjudged Adam. I feel so stupid."

Maxine said, "I guess that puts the ol' kibosh on your love affair."

Greta felt tears rising. "I don't know. He won't be too happy when he learns the real reason I ran out on him."

"So don't tell him. Tell him a bad case of PMS drove you crazy."

Greta shook her head. "Now that we've both made monumental errors in judgment, maybe he'll understand."

"Maybe you can both plead you're only human."

"Maybe."

Maxine said, "You know you came damn close to buying the farm back there?"

"I know. Thanks for coming to my rescue," Greta said. "And I'm really sorry about your car."

Maxine waved her hand, dismissing the problem. "Car, schmar. It can be fixed. But you almost had your brains splattered on the sidewalk. I hope you've learned your lesson and you'll quit playing detective."

Greta finally smiled. "Thanks for caring. I guess I did learn one important thing."

Maxine eyed her suspiciously. "What?"

"Well," Greta said, "no more trying to impress the principal with my dress-for-success wardrobe. The next time I track down a killer, especially in the rain, I'll wear flat shoes and my oldest jeans."

Maxine groaned. "Perfect. Maybe Anne Klein can work attack jeans into her spring line."

Greta pulled Maxine's raincoat tighter around her chest. She was going to feel lousy when all this was over. In fact, she felt lousy already.

Maxine continued to wipe away the steam accumulating on the side window. "Look"—she motioned to Greta—"Pontrelli just shoved Stanley into the patrol car. Ol' Stanley didn't look too happy."

Greta watched the police action going on outside, but then her eye caught a figure running toward them in the rain. It was Adam, sopping wet, looking like he needed a friend or, at least, an explanation.

"Should I go to him?" Greta asked Maxine.

"Why are you asking me? Ten minutes ago you thought he was Jack the Ripper."

"I was wrong."

"Well, don't ask my advice on this one," Maxine insisted. "You know how I feel about consorting with the enemy, though he does look kinda cute with the rain dripping off his lower lip like that."

"The least I can do is invite him in out of the rain."

Maxine made a face. "Why do I have the feeling we saw this scene in a Woody Allen movie?"

Greta rolled her window down partway and waved to Adam. As soon as he spotted her, Adam headed toward Zamora's car.

"Shove over, Max," Greta said. "We have company."